Against the Day

It is 1940 and the Nazis have just invaded Britain.

Frank heard them coming. Crouched in a cellar in the little seaside town of Seabourne, he heard the bombers coming in over the sea, and then the sound of shouts and machine-gun fire in the street.

And now Britain is part of the Third Reich, ruled over by the German military authorities and the ever-present Gestapo. Amidst the shock of invasion and occupation life goes on. Most people keep their heads down. It seems that the fight is over.

Then, almost by chance, Frank and Les are drawn into the secret world of the Resistance. All over Britain there are people who have been quietly prepared—who have been given something 'against the day' that might come: a message, a contact name, a packet of explosive. And when that day does come, the boys find themselves facing the most dangerous time of their lives.

MICHAEL CRONIN is an actor and writer. He has appeared many times on television, on stage, and in films. He is probably best known for *Grange Hill*, where he played Mr Baxter, the gym teacher. Michael lives in South London with his wife and two sons. He has written two television films, *Stealing the Fire* and *No Final Truth*. *Against the Day* is his first novel.

Against the Day

Against the Day

Michael Cronin

Oxford University Press

Oxford New York Toronto

Oxford University Press, Great Clarendon Street, Oxford OX2 6DP

Oxford New York
Athens Auckland Bangkok Bogota
Buenos Aires Calcutta Cape Town Chennai Dar es Salaam
Delhi Florence Hong Kong Istanbul Karachi
Kuala Lumpur Madrid Melbourne
Mexico City Mumbai Nairobi Paris Sao Paulo
Singapore Taipei Tokyo Toronto Warsaw

and associated companies in
Berlin Ibadan

Oxford is a trade mark of Oxford University Press

Copyright © Michael Cronin 1998
First published 1998

A CIP catalogue record for this book is available
from the British Library

Cover illustration: Darren Hayward

ISBN 0 19 271760 X

Printed and bound in Great Britain by
Biddles Ltd, Guildford and King's Lynn

For Jo and Tom and Ben

How it began. 7 September 1940

The first planes appeared high over the sea just after six that evening. Frank Tate ran downstairs to the Residents' Lounge and watched them from the big bay window. Wave after wave, filling the empty blue sky like slow-moving clouds. They were bombers: Dorniers. He recognized their insistent, regular drone and he knew their silhouette from the Enemy Aircraft Guide on the wall of his bedroom. Frank had seen and heard them often these last weeks but never as many as this. It was just like on the newsreels. Just like when the Jerries had invaded Poland. And Norway and Holland and France.

He watched them until he heard the clock in the Civic Gardens strike the half-hour. Then he got up and went to fetch his coat from the stand by the front door. Across the hall, Mr Burford, the proprietor of the guest house, was playing his gramophone: the song about the lilacs and spring and everything being all right—the one he played over and over again.

The Promenade and beach were deserted except for the soldiers patrolling between the Bowling Green and the Pier. One of them waved to him as he hurried by and Frank waved back; it was the corporal, the one from Yorkshire him and his dad always spoke to. In the narrow streets behind the seafront men and women were standing at their doors looking up into the sky. Outside Webber's, the newsagent on the corner, the *Seabourne Messenger*'s placard still read:

AIR BATTLES
OVER THE SOUTH EAST
HEAVY LOSSES

It had said so since the beginning of the week.

Frank waited opposite the bus stop in the High Street until he saw the single-decker come round The Circus and pull up outside Goodenough's, the department store.

His dad waved when he saw him and hurried across the road.

'Frank! What're you doing here?'

'I thought I'd come and meet you.' His dad's old mac, the one he always wore to work, smelt of machine oil. 'Can we have chips tonight, Dad?'

'Yes, I reckon.' Bill Tate looked up and down the street: most shops seemed to have closed already and people were hurrying home. 'Come on,' he said. 'We'll need to get a shift on.'

They had fish and chips, or a saveloy, or just a big bag of chips, two or three times a week. It was easier than doing for themselves back at the guest house: tastier too. Mr Burford had paid off the old woman who cooked the breakfasts and evening meals. 'I can't afford to keep her on,' he'd explained. 'There's no call, Mr Tate. Folk aren't coming to the seaside any more. But I wouldn't want The White Horse Inn to lose you and Frank. I wondered if perhaps you mightn't care to do for yourselves?' So they had. Fry-ups mostly and sometimes a bit of cheese on toast, which they ate in the empty Dining Room still laid with its cloths and cutlery; each table with its hand-written card announcing the room numbers of the guests who had months ago packed their bags and hurried away to the railway station.

But that evening they ate their chips by the railings overlooking the beach. Below them, beyond the barbed wire and tank traps, the pebbles were shifting gently as the tide turned. And beyond the pale line of the surf the sea lay very still, grey and dark like a sheet of metal ribbed with rust in the dying light of the September day.

'It's a big raid,' his dad said, looking up to where the bombers were still advancing darkly from the horizon. 'Some poor beggar'll be taking a hammering. You know I'm fire-watching tonight, don't you?'

The Luftwaffe never bothered with Seabourne. Except the night when the crippled Junkers JU88, hit by the gun batteries dug in along the Downs, had jettisoned its bomb racks over the town. Two houses along the Hove Road had been hit. His dad had been fire-watching that night too. Frank had never seen him look so tired as when he came in next morning. 'Two families, son,' he'd said quietly. 'Just like that. We've been digging all night.'

'D'you have to go, Dad?' he asked. But he knew the answer.

They went inside and cut some rounds of bread and jam for his dad to take with his flask of tea, and one for Frank to take down to the cellar with him.

'Dad?'

'What's that?'

'D'you think the Germans will come tonight?' he asked, which was what he always asked.

And his dad said: 'I wish I knew, Frank,' which was what he always said. He stuffed his flask and sandwiches into his haversack and slung it over his shoulder. 'Come on, old son,' he said, 'into the cage! And I'll see you in the morning.'

The cage was four timber supports and some protective corrugated sheeting which his dad had put together in the cellar. It was where they had found themselves sleeping most nights as the summer of 1940 wore on.

Mr Burford was already there. He was sitting in the striped deckchair wrapped in his old tweed overcoat, and wearing two towels twisted into a turban to protect his head. There was a blanket over his knees; and in his lap he cradled his antique chiming-clock and the attaché case crammed with photographs with which he whiled away the hours till sleep came.

'Hello, Frank,' he said.

'Hello, Mr Burford.' Frank lit the Tate's hurricane lamp and took out his book. It was a Zane Grey cowboy story his dad had recommended. He tried to get into it but it was no use.

'Mr Burford?'

'How's that, Frank?' said Burford, hardly looking up.

'What do you think? About all the bombers.'

'Bombers?'

'Didn't you see them?'

'I can't say I did,' said Burford. And he smiled as he found another memory looking back at him from the photographs spread in his lap. 'I didn't like to look. I mean, it doesn't do any good in the end, does it?'

It was nine o'clock when the bombardment began. Frank always remembered that because Burford's clock began to whirr and strike the hour with its clear, silvery chime. And suddenly the cellar was filled with noise. Relentless, roaring, ear-splitting noise that made his ears ring and his head pound: the thunder of the guns,

and the shriek of shells that followed so closely one
after the other they became a single, prolonged scream.
Hour after hour. Huddled beneath his blanket he lost
all sense of time. All sense of anything—except the
fear. The fear that he was going to die there
underneath The White Horse Inn. On his own.

And then suddenly, as suddenly as they had begun,
the guns fell silent.

'Mr Burford?'

'Is that you, Frank?' came the barely audible reply.

'Why have they stopped?'

But before Burford could answer there was a
deafening explosion not far off. The beach? And then
another closer still. The walls of the cellar shook and
dust and plaster fell from the ceiling. In the room
above they heard the windows shatter as machine-guns
raked the front of the house. Rifle fire began to open
up in all directions: savage staccato bursts and the
answering clatter of heavier weapons. There were
shouts, silences, and shouting again as the battle raged.
The flame of Frank's hurricane lamp was reduced to a
flicker and finally went out altogether, adding its acrid
fumes to the musty closeness of the cellar. When
Burford's lamp ran out they would be in complete
darkness. Frank pulled the blanket over his head and
waited.

The noise must have done something to his ears
because he wasn't sure exactly when the fighting
stopped. Only that, little by little, he was aware that he
could hear again: the sound of his heart; the precise
tick of Burford's clock; water hissing in a pipe nearby;
and then . . . Was it? It sounded like lorries moving
along the Promenade outside.

Was it over? He pulled the blanket from his head. At

the far end of the cellar thin shafts of grey light were drifting in through the lid of the coal-hole.

'Mr Burford?' he whispered. 'Mr Burford?'

Gordon Burford was slumped sideways in his deckchair. His eyes were closed and his mouth gaped pinkly in his pale, dust-covered face. The clock still lay in his lap, but the case of photographs had fallen open and its contents were scattered on the floor at his feet.

Frank threw off the blanket and stumbled up the cellar steps. He tugged at the handle of the door. It was stuck. Stuck fast. Something must have fallen against it in the hallway on the other side. Try as he might it wouldn't budge.

'Frank?'

'Mr Burford!' He spun round peering down into the gloom. 'I thought . . . I thought you were . . . '

'Praying, Frank. I've been praying all the time.'

'I can't get it open, Mr Burford. Please help me.'

'Whatever for?'

'I've got to get out.'

'But we mustn't, Frank. We mustn't do that.'

'But I've got to find Dad!' Frank stumbled back down the steps and across the cellar floor. 'He's at the factory. He was fire-watching at Bell's Precision.'

'But they'll kill you. Don't go, Frank.' Burford was on his feet, shuffling towards him, the blanket caught between his legs. 'Don't leave me here, Frank. I can't get through there. I won't let you . . . I won't!'

But Frank had already thrown back the lid and was clambering up through the coal-hole and into the silence of the yard outside.

Everything was so still. And everything was still there. The guest houses on either side were still there: the Connaught and the Palm Court. There were seagulls sitting on the roofs across the alley. It was all just the same. Except for the smell of burning. And the pebbles—there were pebbles everywhere.

'Dad?' he called. 'Dad, where are you?'

And he started to run.

Chapter 1

'Look at you!'

'What?' Colin had just come in from out-the-back and was struggling with his braces.

'You look wore out before you start.'

'I can't sleep, ma,' he said. 'I've told you that before. Not with Frank in the room.'

Edie Worth took the comb from the mantelpiece and began to drag it through her son's hair. 'What's he done now?' she said.

'He's making noises again.'

'Dreaming?'

'Talking to himself. Ow!' Colin pulled away, rubbing the top of his head. 'He keeps me awake, ma. It's not fair.'

'There's plenty that's not fair in this world, my lad. The sooner you realize that the happier you'll be. Now get yourself off to school.'

'What about Frank?'

'If Frank Tate wants to be late for school that's his look-out.'

When Colin had gone Edie put her hand to the pot. It was still warm—just. As she sat and sipped the dark tea she looked around the room: the big old range, the rods of washing hung above it to dry, the glass-fronted cabinet crammed with her mother's bits and pieces of china, and the sink that was always full these days—like the cottage itself. And she tried to picture her own kitchen in the poky terraced house in Swindon. It wasn't much but it had been hers. And Len's. Still would be if it hadn't been for the blessed war. Now her husband was a prisoner of war somewhere in France she couldn't even pronounce and she was back in the cottage in Shevington where she'd been born. It wasn't fair.

There were footsteps on the stairs and Frank pushed open the door and sat down at the table.

'Good morning, Auntie Edie,' she said caustically.

'Morning.'

She watched him as he spread his bread with marge. He was the same age as Colin, they'd been born within a couple of months of each other. But that was where the likeness ended. Frank Tate was spoilt. Her brother Bill had ruined his only son. What with that and the life the two of them had led, hand to mouth, never in the same place six months at a time, rooms and boarding-houses, it was little wonder he was such a handful.

'You been dreaming again?'

'No,' he said, and folded his bread into a sandwich. But he had. In his dream—it was the one he'd had before—he had been out looking for his dad. All over Seabourne, all along the seafront, on the pier, up the High Street. Then, as he was crossing the Municipal Bowling Green, he saw the old macintosh, the one just like his dad used to wear, lying in the gully at the edge of the neatly-trimmed grass. Just an old mac. Until he went closer and saw the slippered feet and pyjama trousers. It wasn't his dad; it was an old man. He had never seen a dead person before but he knew that that was what he was: he had a discarded look, just as though someone had thrown him away. His panama hat lay next to him. There was a dark, oval bruise on his temple. His eyes were open and were glaring accusingly at the big, white pebble on the grass beside his head. There were pebbles everywhere.

'You kept Colin awake,' said his aunt.

'No I never.'

That was his father! That was her brother Bill all over. The first thing Bill Tate always did was deny it—

9

whatever it was. 'Yes, you did, my lad! And you know it. You were chattering away half the night.'

Frank picked up his slice and headed for the door.

'And where do you think you're going?'

'School.'

'You're going to get that copper lit for me before you do. I've got a basket of laundry to start the minute I've finished this mouthful of tea.'

The third match got the newspaper spills to light but it wasn't much of a flame. He'd be late again. She was always finding chores for him to do last thing. Anything to make his life a misery.

The checkpoint on the village green was unpredictable: that was the point, of course. You never knew when they'd stop you. And Frank was relieved as he came running down the lane to see that the barrier was raised. But then, as he approached, the guard—the one they called 'Bumpsadaisy'—stepped from the sentries' hut and held up his hand.

Frank pulled out his Identity Card and waited. The soldier frowned at it, comparing the photograph with the boy, the way he always did.

'You are twelve years old,' he said. 'I have a boy like you. He is twelve years old.'

But Frank said nothing. He never did.

'Bumpsadaisy' turned to his companions in the hut. '*Dieser, der mag uns nicht,*' he said. And Hans and 'Knees' laughed. 'You don't like us,' he said, bringing his face close to Frank's. But Frank didn't budge. The soldier shook his head. 'You are very stubborn,' he said, handing back the card. 'And you are late for school, I think.'

Warden Firth put down her thick blue pencil and stretched her aching fingers. There was always so much to be done. And these days it always had to be done: 'At once!' But that was the way SS Hauptsturmführer

Honegger liked things done. The Head of Security at Shevington Hall—Head of Security! And he couldn't be more than thirty, if that—was not a man with time to spare. She looked out at the garden beyond her window. It had to be confessed, it had a rather neglected air. But it couldn't be helped. There were more important things in her life now than tidy borders and rose cuttings.

Betty Firth had volunteered for the position of Village Warden because, as she had told the meeting summoned to the village hall within days of the Germans arriving, 'I love Shevington. And I want us to get back to normal as quickly as possible. I'm convinced it can be done and done without any unpleasantness. The authorities,' she had turned to acknowledge politely the Wehrmacht officer and his colleague with whom she shared the platform, 'have drawn up the rules by which we can do so. I want to play my part, ladies and gentlemen. You all know me and know I will always do so to the very best of my ability.'

They did all know her. She had always been a busybody. And now the Jerries had given her an armband and a telephone in her back sitting room to make it official. Now she had the right—and more power than even poor old Dick Carr, the village bobby—to be nosy. And she could always be counted on to be so to the very best of her ability.

In the kitchen she poured boiling water over the gauze bag of camomile flowers and watched the water colour in the bottom of the cup.

Back to normal. More or less. Six months, that was all it had taken. And it had been achieved with remarkable ease. One heard such horrid stories from elsewhere of what the Invasion and Occupation had brought. But Shevington had weathered the storm. There had been changes, that was inevitable. One or two new faces, of course. Edith Tate, Worth as she was now, was back at her mother's with her children: the boy, and the older girl who worked up at the Hall. The father, not a local

11

man, had been captured at Dunkirk. Yes, Nan Tate certainly had a houseful what with the Worths and that other grandson of hers, the one who'd been orphaned: Bill Tate's son.

There had been losses, of course. But thankfully things hadn't lasted long enough for there to be too many. The two younger Cowdrey brothers. And Henry Underwood, the headmaster's son. And Tom Barlow— he'd lost an arm. It was very sad but it didn't do to dwell on such things. What else was there of note? Well, there were those two guttersnipes out at Keeper Thrale's. So typical of Vera Thrale to take in a pair like that: the big, pasty-faced girl and her runt of a brother. Gill was their name. Incorrigible cockney types. Products of the darkest East End.

Betty took her cup and went back into the office. While she was away the cat, Gargery, had slipped through the open window and was curled up in the big, wheel-backed chair opposite her desk.

The pile of letters to be censored had diminished appreciably since her early start that morning. At first she'd felt rather awkward listening to her neighbours' correspondence—that was how she thought of it: she knew them all so well she could hear their voices as she read them. But, finally, she'd come to the conclusion that wardenship demanded a certain detachment; and that whining and ill-considered remarks about the authorities didn't help the situation and did call for constant monitoring. And, in time, she was able to wield her blue indelible pencil without hesitation.

She sat down at her desk again. But before resuming her duties, she opened the envelope marked CONFIDENTIAL COMMUNICATION and re-read the letter which had arrived from the Hall earlier that morning. SECRET, it said at the top. And was signed by General von Schreier himself, the man in charge of the whole of the Southern Area Command. As a child

Betty had always loved secrets; they were dangerous and demanding; but it was so nice to be trusted. When she'd finished, she slipped the letter back in its envelope and locked it carefully in the drawer of her desk. It would never do for unauthorized eyes to read it.

'That would spoil the surprise, wouldn't it, Gargery?' she said. And the cat blinked back at her.

Besides, everyone would know soon enough. The announcement would be made public in a couple of days. Such a surprise. And there would be so much to do. Still, forewarned was forearmed.

From the framed photograph above the desk Adolf Hitler's demanding gaze met hers.

'Getting on,' she said.

And picking up her pencil she went back to work.

The Gills, Les and Mill, had arrived in Shevington not long after Frank Tate. During the confused weeks that followed the Invasion the roads had been crowded with refugees, and no one had taken much notice when the ragged boy and girl came trudging along the Patfield Road pushing their battered pram. They had walked right through the village and were not far from the Hall when they stopped at Keeper Thrale's.

When General von Schreier made Shevington Hall his private residence, Sir Quentin Demeger had gone north to one of his family's estates in Derbyshire. But Sir Quentin's staff had stayed. What else was there to do? Most of them had worked at the Hall all their lives. Alec Thrale had walked its woods and fields as long as he could remember.

When Vera Thrale opened the door she saw a big, strong girl with a plain, honest face, who looked about fifteen years old and who certainly wasn't 'village'—her husband would never have allowed anyone from the village in the house—and a small boy with a mop of unruly black hair. Mill and Les saw a tall young woman wearing a threadbare silk dressing-gown secured at the waist with a man's tie.

'Any chance of a drink of water, missis?' asked Mill.

'You're from London!' said Vera, smiling.

'Yes,' said Mill.

'You look exhausted.'

'I ain't, but he is,' said Mill quickly. 'He's my brother.'

'Come inside.'

And that was it. Mill was given a bed in the attic; and Les a mattress and blankets in the shed across the yard.

It was where he and Frank retreated most evenings to lick their wounds among the battered suitcases and rusting garden-tools. Frank had spent ten minutes after school that afternoon trying to explain to Miss Meacher that it was his Aunt Edie who had made him late again. He was still doing so.

'I told her, Les,' he said. 'I told her it was Edie's fault.'

'Wasting your breath, Frank,' his friend replied. 'You ought to know that by now.'

'I know.' Frank sat down on the battered suitcase at the end of Les's mattress. 'Les?'

'What?'

Frank sighed. 'Oh, I don't know.'

'Don't take no notice—I don't.'

'Edie, Miss Meacher, all of 'em, they're always having a go at me. What's the matter with people?'

'People do—they like having a go at each other.'

'But it's worse now; it's worse since the Jerries came. Haven't you noticed that? People are arguing with each other all the time.'

'Keep your head down—that's what you want to do. I do.'

He did. Which was peculiar for someone who looked like a really tough nut. It was the one thing Frank found hard to cope with where Les was concerned. In every other way they were the best of friends. At first it was being outsiders that had thrown them together. Neither of them being particularly welcomed by the village kids. Then, as the months passed, they became inseparable. Two of a kind. But when it came to speaking up or having a go Les couldn't have been more unlike Frank.

'The fact is, Les, people didn't ought to be arguing with each other,' Frank said impatiently. 'The only ones people ought to be arguing with are the Nasties.'

Les shook his head. 'Leave off, eh! Only mugs argues with the Nasties. You fancy seeing off that white-haired geezer up at the Hall, do you—the SS Nasty? Don't be silly!'

The door from the yard opened and Mill Gill came in and closed it quickly behind her.

''Lo, Frank,' she said.

''Lo, Mill.'

She sat down on an upturned box and took a crumpled cigarette from the pocket of her apron. 'What're you looking so miserable about?' she said.

'Everything,' said Frank.

'Oh, is that all.' She lit the cigarette and inhaled luxuriously. 'Me and Vera's been spring-cleaning,' she said. 'Here! She was only dancing in the kitchen, wasn't she! With a feather duster. Never a dull moment with Vera.'

'What was she dancing for?'

Mill laughed. 'She says you don't need a reason. And what's the matter with you, Les? You look like you lost a pound and found a tanner.'

Frank and Les watched her as she tried very carefully to blow a smoke-ring. It didn't work; it never did. 'One of these days,' she said. 'Oh, cheer up, you two, for heaven's sake; you look a right pair of Jonahs.'

'It's this place,' said Frank. 'It's just Shevington and everything.'

'You don't know when you're well off, neither of you. There's plenty would be grateful living in a place like this.'

15

'Come off it, Mill. Nothing ever happens here. Nobody ever does anything!'

'What's people supposed to do, then—according to Frank Tate?'

'I don't know. Pay them back for a start.'

'Pay who back?'

'The Jerries, who else? Do something to . . . I don't know.'

'Listen to it! You want your bloody head read, you do. Do what, then?'

'Something. Not just sit back and let them do what they like. Like the night the soldiers took Cec Warwick and his family away. Yes, and burned their caravan. Remember that? 'Cos they was gypsies. What about that? Nobody did anything about that. Nobody even talks about it any more.'

'They took 'em away somewhere to re-settle 'em. They said so.'

'They burned their caravan, Mill! And smashed everything. My gran said Cec and his family been travelling these roads for years. People knew them, Mill. But nobody said anything or tried to help them. They just let the Jerries do it to them. That's what I mean.'

'Look, Frank,' said Mill, 'people's took a hammering. They just want a quiet life.'

'But if nobody ever does anything, Mill, it's . . . it's like they've won.'

'Who?'

'The Jerries!'

'Gawd, Frank—they *have* won!'

Frank shrugged. 'Still don't mean . . . look, it don't mean we can't go on hoping.'

'Here we go again.'

'Consider Garibaldi!'

'You and your Garibaldi! What's Garibaldi got to do with it?'

'Because Garibaldi never gave up.' It had been not long after Frank arrived at Nan Tate's, not long after

16

he'd told her about his dad and everything, that his grandmother had pointed to the picture on the wall by the kitchen door: the big, bearded man with the red shirt, his arms folded, gazing steadfastly into the sun. Always consider Garibaldi, Frank, she'd told him; I set great store by that picture. That was your grandfather's picture. He'd thought she meant it was a picture of his grandfather and had asked her if Garibaldi was an Irish name. No, she said, it was Italian; Garibaldi was Italian. He'd found out the rest by sneaking a look at Colin's encyclopaedia, the one his cousin didn't allow anyone else to look at: 'Guiseppe Garibaldi, 1807–1882, patriot, soldier, and fighter for freedom'. He'd been captured, condemned to death, escaped, captured again, loads of times. Italy, South America, Italy again. And Garibaldi had never given up; he just kept going. But, then, you only had to look at his face to see that. 'It's a fact, Mill. Garibaldi never gave up hoping and I ain't either.'

'People want a quiet life and you can't blame them. Be fair, Frank.'

'Why?'

' 'Cos you have to be, that's why.'

'I don't know about that.'

'I do then. And there's something else I know: if you go looking for trouble them Nazis'll give it you, good and proper!'

'I know that.'

'You don't—you don't know when you're well off. I told you, there's plenty would be grateful living somewhere as quiet as this place. I am. And you are, ain't you, Les?'

'Leave off, Mill, eh? He only said—'

'Look, Mill,' said Frank, 'all I'm saying is you can't help . . . you can't help hoping, wanting something to happen, that's all.'

Mill stood up; she knew that when Frank Tate was in one of his Garibaldi moods there was no shifting him. 'I daresay,' she said, pinching the end from her cigarette and putting it back in the pocket of her pinny. 'Well,

17

some of us have got work to do. Vera will be wondering where I am. Ta-ta. And just you behave yourselves.'

'Not much else we can do, is there?' said Frank.

Warden Firth filled the best chair in Nan Tate's tiny kitchen: a large, smiling presence with apple-cheeks and cornflower-blue eyes that didn't miss a thing.

'Well, I certainly expect a delivery soon, Edith,' she said. 'But, as I'm sure you understand, the channels are chock-a-block with high-priority important correspondence seven days a week; and letters from prisoners of war do have to take their place in the queue.'

'Yes, I understand that, Miss Firth,' said Edie. 'Only it's—'

'I don't think people actually appreciate what a triumph of organization it is simply keeping all that paper on the move.'

'We do, Miss Firth. Only it's just that we look forward so much to hearing from Len.'

'I know you do, dear. And let's hope you have him home soon. Just as soon as everything's been sorted out. Wouldn't you like to have your dad home again, Colin?' she said, beaming across the table to where Colin was sitting with his *New Scouting Manual* open in front of him.

'Yes, I would, Miss Firth,' he replied.

'Of course you would! A boy needs his father. Just look at master Frank: I can't help thinking it's want of a father's discipline made that boy such a handful. Never out of trouble, it seems. Oh, it makes my blood boil, it does! And when you think what young people have waiting for them, eh, Edith? Not like in our day.'

'No, Miss Firth.'

'Are you looking to the future, Colin?'

'All the time, Miss Firth.'

'That's the spirit! There's absolutely no excuse for

pessimism or negative behaviour. Well, now!' The Warden turned quickly as the back door opened. 'Here's the very chap whose name was this moment on our lips. And how are you, Frank Tate?'

Frank glared at her. She was sitting with her legs stretched between him and the table: there was no way past.

'Keeping out of mischief, I hope?' she said. 'Well, I never, Edith—I do believe the cat's got his tongue.'

'He's in one of his moods, Miss Firth—don't take any notice.'

'I don't, dear. I'm afraid we've no time for moods. There's far too much to do. Construction and Co-operation, those are the watchwords! That's what will put everything back together again. The last time I was up in London there were British workmen and German soldiers working side by side clearing away all the dreadful rubble and destruction. Do you know, there are parts of that great city where you wouldn't know there had been a war. Onwards! As a matter of fact, that is going to be the theme for—Oh, there!' Betty Firth clamped her hand over her mouth dramatically. 'There, you almost made me give it away.'

'Give what away, Miss Firth?' asked Colin.

'No!' she replied, giggling. 'Not another word will you get out of me, Colin Worth! It's in my special, confidential drawer and that's where it's going to stay till the time comes. Though I will say this—I think we're all in for something of a surprise. There. And your mother, Edith?' she said suddenly. 'Where's Nan Tate this evening?'

'Nan's still out,' said Colin.

'On that bicycle of hers? She really is indefatigable, isn't she!'

'She shouldn't be on a bike at all at her age,' said Edie. 'I've told her time and time again.'

'Yes. She must be an awful worry to you, Edith. They can be so stubborn, can't they—the elderly? I know father used to—'

19

'Nan ain't stubborn.'

The Warden turned to look at Frank, who had remained standing in the doorway. 'I was speaking, thank you, young man,' she said.

'Nan goes out on her bike because she always has,' said Frank angrily. 'She always has and nobody's going to stop her not for all their checkpoints and the rest of it.'

Warden Firth looked away. 'So very contrary,' she said.

'I don't think mother means any harm, Miss Firth,' said Edie quickly.

'I didn't mean Nan Tate in particular, Edith. I was simply reflecting that no matter how helpful or sensible a thing may be, if it comes from the Authorities there are always one or two who'll take a contrary line and won't be at all grateful.'

'What have I got to be grateful for?' demanded Frank. 'I haven't got anything to be grateful for.'

'Frank!' said Edie. 'Behave!'

'No. I ain't going to be grateful to the Germans,' he said. 'Why should I? They killed my dad!' And pushing past the astonished Warden, he made off along the passage and up the stairs.

'Frank?' Edie called. 'Frank, you come back here this minute!'

Betty Firth got up, buttoning her coat. 'One tries to be understanding,' she said. 'But it's more than time Master Frank Tate began to take stock of himself.'

'I'm so sorry, Miss Firth.'

'We are none of us given unlimited rope.'

'Of course not,' said Edie, following her to the back door.

The Warden paused, confronting the picture on the wall beside the door. 'Still there, I see,' she said. 'Despite the fact that I have asked for it to be removed on several occasions.'

'Only it's mother's favourite, you see,' said Edie.

'That's as maybe. It is inappropriate, Edith. I've told her that. I have offered a replacement; that offer still stands.'

And was likely to go on standing, thought Edie. Perhaps Nan could be persuaded to take Garibaldi down but to put Adolf Hitler up was another thing altogether. 'I'll make sure I remind her, Miss Firth,' she said. 'And you will let us know the minute anything comes from Len, won't you?'

'Of course.'

'Thank you, Miss Firth. Say goodnight to Miss Firth, Colin.'

'Goodnight, Miss Firth.'

'Goodnight, Colin. Goodnight, Edith.'

Chapter 2

'What's that lot, Mill?' asked Les.

'It's apples, ennit,' she said. 'Shift yourself!' And she dumped the wooden box on the kitchen table.

Mill fed Les on his own most mornings. Keeper Thrale himself came and went at all hours of the day and night; and Vera seldom sat down to a meal.

'Looks like a lot of old newspapers,' he said.

'That's what she's wrapped them in. They've been in the cellar. She wants me to see that they ain't gone pinky or nothing.' She sniffed the apple she'd unwrapped. 'This one looks all right.'

'It's the ones on the bottom will have gone pinky.'

'Yeah, I s'pose. 'Struth,' she said. 'Look at this.' She smoothed the crumpled newspaper flat and read: 'Seventh of September 1940. Here, that was just about the time the Jerries come, wasn't it?'

'It was a Saturday,' said Les, wiping his plate with his bread.

'You ever think about them days, Les?'

'What—the fighting and that?'

'No,' his sister said quietly. 'Them bloody Crockers.'

'Them? Nah,' said Les. But he did. And he knew she did too. 'They en't worth the trouble.'

She unwrapped another apple and inspected it. 'Les?'

'What?'

'You know what Frank said the other day—you know, about doing something and that? You won't, will you?'

'Leave off, Mill, eh?'

'I'm serious, Les. You wouldn't do nothing stupid, would you?'

''Course not.'

'And don't you let him go talking you into something, d'you hear? You know the way he goes on about things. Like a gramophone record. You know what we agreed. To keep our heads down. To keep out of trouble. Are you listening?'

'I ain't stupid.'

'No, not much you ain't.'

'I ain't.'

'It's important, Les. You know what I mean.'

'I know. You don't have to go on at me.'

'Here,' she said, tossing him an apple. 'Stick that in your pocket quick.'

'What d'you think you're doing with that box, girl?'

Les slipped the apple into his pocket as he and Mill turned to find Alec Thrale standing in the doorway from the yard. The gamekeeper was a big, bearded man whose calling had trained him to move quietly and easily. He carried his shotgun, and his game-bag was slung from his shoulder. He ducked in quickly under the lintel and threw the bag on to the table.

'I asked you a question.'

'I got them out the cellar,' said Mill. 'Mrs Thrale wanted me to see they was all right.'

'They're all right.' Alec began to re-wrap the apples Mill had taken from the box and put them back with the rest. 'And I don't want them touched. Now put the box back where you found it,' he said. When he saw them looking at him, he added, 'They're Egremonts. Russets. They're particular favourites of mine.'

'Right ho, Mr Thrale.'

'Now, if you please.'

Mill picked up the box and started back to the cellar.

'What about you?' said Thrale, turning to Les. 'Isn't there something you're supposed to be doing?'

'Going to school,' said Les.

'Go on, then. And when you get there, make sure you give that apple in your pocket to the teacher.'

Eyes in the back of his head, thought Les, as he went across the yard. Gamekeepers were as bad as policemen. He waited until he was clear of the house then pulled out the apple and looked at it. It was a brown, leathery-looking thing. His favourite, was it? He bit into it. And couldn't see what all the fuss was about. Funny cove. They both were—him and her: Vera never stopped talking and him, Alec, hardly ever had two words together for anybody. Still, the Thrales weren't the worst. Les and Mill couldn't really have found a better or a safer billet. Few people ever ventured into Keeper Thrale's yard; they knew his temper too well. Mill was right: it would be just stupid to get into any sort of bother and ruin it all. But it was hard: keeping your head down. Very hard. And with Frank always going on the way he did. There'd been a couple of times in the last months when he'd wanted to tell him the truth. But it wasn't his secret to tell; it was Mill's as well. And he never had.

Les took a last bite from the apple, drew back his arm, and threw it as hard as he could into the wood. Then he clambered over the stile and set off down the lane to school.

Alec Thrale placed his shotgun in the rack, slipped the chain through its trigger-guard, and turned the key in the padlock. General von Schreier had insisted that whenever the gun was not in use it must be safely secured. Or rather, it was the General's SS advisers who had insisted: civilian firearms had been confiscated early in the Occupation, and there were one or two up at the Hall who felt strongly that Keeper Thrale's weapon should have been no exception. But the General had overridden them. He'd explained to them that no gamekeeper could do his job without his shotgun. He was a man who understood such things: his family owned large estates on the Polish border.

Alec sat down—he had been out since first light checking his nesting-sites—and taking out his pouch, filled the bowl of his pipe. It was a mixture Vera had concocted for him from leaf she'd grown and dried the previous year and one or two of her garden herbs. It was a bit light and aromatic but Alec didn't complain: tobacco of any sort was a luxury. He watched the smoke drift over his head and mingle with the traps and cages suspended from the roof. He had known this outhouse all his life. He had watched his father at that workbench; he'd sat here and learnt the workings of the shotgun which, with his father's death, had finally become his own. His father had taught him all there was to know, walking the woods and fields night and day, season by season, until there was no one knew them better than Sam Thrale's boy, Alec. And it was a knowledge you couldn't find in books or maps. Which was probably why they chose him in the first place. He always thought of them as 'they'; but, the fact of the matter was, there had only ever been one of them.

It was some time towards the end of June 1940, not long after the fall of France, that he'd taken his shotgun into Willoughby's, the gunsmith's in Patfield, for old man Willoughby to give it the once-over. The following week, when he went in again to collect it, there had been a chap standing at the counter talking to the old man: smartly-dressed, well-spoken, civilian tweeds but with an obvious military bearing. From his conversation it was evident he knew his guns. He seemed to know Alec, too: or, at least, he knew Sir Quentin Demeger's keeper by name and reputation. Carey, he said his name was; and invited Alec for a drink before he caught the bus back to Shevington. They'd crossed the square and gone into the Market Place Hotel where Carey was staying. They chatted—or rather, Carey had—about this and that. Dunkirk, of course; and what Carey described as the humiliating defeat of the British Expeditionary Force and its allies. Then, after another drink, he'd said quite casually, 'Tell me, Mr Thrale, do you consider yourself a patriot? You may, of course, tell me to go to the devil, but the reason I ask is that I'd like to make you a proposition. To be painfully frank, it is a proposition of last resort, a proposition coincident with our defeat. Singular men, Mr Thrale, that's who I'm looking for. Men like yourself—solitary men who can be secret: sentinels, storehouses, messengers, men who know their country and love it. Are you such a man, Mr Thrale?' They'd met again a few days later not far from Patfield Palace, the ruined Roman villa out along the Patfield Road; and Carey had handed him four hand-grenades and a small box of explosives. 'And what do I do with these?' Alec had asked. 'When the time comes you'll be contacted,' Carey had told him. 'In the meantime, I ask you simply to keep them safe. Against the day, Mr Thrale. Good luck to you.' Alec had never seen him again. The Invasion had come. And the Surrender. But no contact had ever been made. Alec had often wondered in the months that followed if perhaps Carey was dead. And if there were other 'singular men' just like himself up and down the country who had been approached by other 'Careys' and who were like him still waiting—against the day.

He knocked out his pipe and stood up. It was getting on for nine o'clock and that young chap Ted Naylor, from Middelbury, was supposed to be coming over that morning with a quote for the new rearing-pens. And locking the outhouse door securely, the keeper went in for his breakfast.

From the top of the churchyard wall you could see right across the playground. It was where Frank and Les always sat at playtimes or before the bell rang in the mornings.

'I've got an idea,' said Frank. 'You know, about what to do. I've been thinking really hard.'

Les nodded. He was watching George Poole and Wally Carr and the rest of them, who were playing football at the other end of the schoolyard. They could go for weeks just leaving him and Frank to their own devices; but then, without any warning, like now, like when it seemed they were just playing football, they would come and start something that usually ended in a fight and Les and Frank getting the blame. The good thing was, whenever that happened and they sent a letter home with him, Vera went off alarming—not at him but the people at the school. It was good that.

' 'Cos we've got to do something, Les. Nobody else is. To show the Jerries they can't just . . . you know. Les, are you listening?'

'Yes,' he said. 'Frank? What was that your nan told you about Vera and old Thrale? You know, where she came from and that?'

'What, about her dad and the other professors? I told you, they bought some land the other side of Datcham years ago. They all lived together in a big house. Nan knew all about it; she always does. She said they used wooden ploughs and had looms and things for making their own clothes. She said they ought to have known better, being educated people.'

'I s'pose that'd account for it. You know, Vera being such a case and that.'

'I s'pose so.'

'And what about old Thrale?'

'Never mind him . . . Look out,' said Frank quietly, 'here comes the Toff.'

A young man in his early twenties, bespectacled, and rather anxious-looking, was hurrying across the yard towards them. The Toff, Mr Peter Sims, was the youngest of the three teachers at Shevington School. By the time he reached the wall he was out of breath. 'Ah,' he said, 'Tate and . . . Tate and Gill. You—'

But the rest of what he said was drowned out by the sound of the assembly bell ringing as Miss Meacher appeared on the school steps and summoned them inside.

Frank and Les jumped down from the wall.

'What is it, sir?' said Frank.

'You're . . . rather, you were, sitting on the wall,' said the teacher, scooping his fingers nervously through his thinning hair.

'We have to, sir,' said Frank.

'But it's not allowed. I've told you so countless times. You could fall backwards into the churchyard. It's dangerous.'

'Not half as dangerous as being in the same yard as George Poole and his Nazis.'

'What? Oh, don't be ridiculous, Tate; they are nothing of the sort. Now, look here, I shan't tell you again . . . about the wall. All right?'

'Right ho, sir,' said Les. 'Come on, Frank.'

'Useless, that's what he is,' said Frank, looking back to where the teacher was standing. 'Just like all the rest of them.'

As Mr Underwood, the headmaster, took his place at the end of the hall Miss Meacher clapped her hands for silence. Mr Sims stood beside her, frowning and polishing his spectacles on his handkerchief.

'Good morning, boys and girls,' said the headmaster.

'Good morning, Mr Underwood,' they chorused.

He held up a large brown envelope for everyone to see. 'This envelope,' he told them, 'was delivered to me yesterday, together with an instruction that I am to open it this morning at nine o'clock precisely and read you its contents. Similar envelopes will then be opened in schools throughout the kingdom . . . ah, country. At nine o'clock precisely.'

All eyes turned to the clock on the wall above him; there was less than a minute to go.

'Making a song and a dance about it, isn't he?' whispered Frank.

'It's one of them Nazi letters,' said Les.

The minute-hand fell into place. The headmaster opened the envelope and took out a sheet of paper. He cleared his throat and read:

' "From: The Ministry of Home Affairs
             Department of Education
             Queens Anne's Gate
             LONDON

                           7th April 1941

To the Staff and Pupils of All British Schools

It is my privilege to inform you that Sunday the 20th of April 1941 is the occasion of the birthday of Reichsführer Adolf Hitler. On that day ceremonies of Thanksgiving and Celebration will take place throughout the New Europe." '

Mr Underwood paused, looking down at the sheet of paper in his hand. Then, almost imperceptibly, he squared his shoulders and read on:

' "All staff and pupils will be required to take part in the festivities and celebratory events which will be organized in collaboration with their local communities; and which will be centred on a broadcast by the Führer direct from Berlin and transmitted to cities, towns, and villages throughout the New Europe.

            Dr Jürgen Brandt
            Controller of Education

            Heil Hitler." '

Mr Underwood lowered the sheet of paper and looked down at the faces staring up at him from the hall. He knew that they were waiting for him to speak, to tell them, to give them some explanation of what it all meant and how it came to be: the way he usually did, the way teachers were supposed to. But he had no explanation to give them. Twenty-five years before he had fought in the great 'war to end all wars'—he had a medal in a drawer at home to say he had done so with particular courage; he had seen the sons, husbands, and brothers of Shevington die in the mud of Flanders. But despite the horror of it all he had returned with the belief that some good would come of it, and that those men had not died in vain, if generations to come might be spared the terrible demands of the madness known as war. But the madness had come again, within a generation, his son's generation; and it had taken his only child and humiliated and enslaved his country. And now the madman himself was writing to invite them to his birthday party. Who could possibly explain such a thing?

'Children,' he began. But no words came.

'Shall I, headmaster?' said Miss Meacher quietly.

'Thank you,' he said.

'It doesn't leave us very much time, does it, children?' she said. 'Even so, I'm sure Shevington School will not be found wanting when it comes to making the 20th of April a day to . . . to remember.' And now it was Miss Meacher who seemed lost for words.

In the silence a lorry drew up at the checkpoint across the Green and through the open windows they could hear the German driver laughing with 'Bumpsadaisy' and the other guards.

'Shall I begin the register, headmaster?' she asked.

'By all means, Miss Meacher.' As she did so, Mr Underwood turned to Mr Sims. 'An historic occasion, Mr Sims.'

The young teacher slipped his spectacles over his ears and peered back at him. 'Historic, headmaster? Oh, yes—yes, indeed! We should have no doubt of that.'

'I haven't, Mr Sims; I have no doubt at all.'

And with that, Mr Underwood stepped from the platform and walked slowly out of the hall.

'He's took it bad,' said Les, watching him go.

''Course he has,' said Frank. ''Cos it's too much to bear, that's why! How can anybody celebrate Hitler's birthday?'

'Dressin' up and that?' said Les.

'What?'

'That's what they usually do, ennit.'

'Don't be daft, Les. What, you mean a pageant or something? With kings and queens and Nelson, that sort of thing? They can't do that for Hitler, can they?'

'Well, it don't matter. 'Cos they'll tell us what we got to do, won't they? It'll come in one of them brown envelopes—it always does.'

'But celebrating for him! That's like having him here.'

'Frank Tate, stop that talking!' On the platform Miss Meacher was glaring at him over the top of the register.

It would, it would be like Hitler actually being here, thought Frank. And that was something even Hitler hadn't dared do. Though people wondered why. Why, instead of setting a triumphant foot on English soil, he had summoned the New British Government to meet him in Berlin. It had been on all the newsreels; the Mobile Film Unit had shown it in the village hall. There were rumours, of course. People said he had come. That he came often. They said he came at dead of night and drove round and round the empty streets of London with his cronies, laughing and carrying on. He'd been seen. That was what people said.

'It's too much to bear, Les,' Frank whispered, as they filed out of assembly. 'We've got to do something now. And I know just what.'

They stood in the shadow of the ruined barn and looked across the road to the boundary wall of Shevington Hall. It wasn't more than seven or eight feet high and there was thick ivy almost to the top.

'But what about the other side?' said Les. 'We got to get back out again.'

31

'Come on, Les. We've got to try.'

'If they catch us there'll be hell to pay. The Nasties don't mess about.'

'They won't catch us. They don't expect anybody to do something like this. All right, I'll go on my own, then.'

'No, I'll come. It's just . . . It don't matter.'

'Come on, then!'

They scrambled down the bank and were halfway across the road when the patrol lorry came careering round the corner. The driver slammed his fist against the horn and sent Frank and Les scampering desperately back up the bank. The lorry sped by in a cloud of dust. They could hear the soldiers in the back laughing.

'That was too bloomin' close, Frank!'

'But that's good,' said Frank. 'Don't you see? It means they won't be past again for ages. Come on.'

On the other side of the wall the undergrowth was dense and overgrown. But they pushed their way through and were soon in the woods. After a few minutes the trees began to thin out and they had their first glimpse of the gardens and imposing country house half a mile and more away. The woods stretched down the hill almost to the edge of the lawns and boxed hedges, the ornamental pond, and the broad flight of steps which rose to the terrace at the back of Shevington Hall, General Gunther von Schreier's personal residence and headquarters.

'Like a palace, isn't it?' said Frank. And crept forward.

'Where are you going?'

'I want to get closer.'

'What for?'

'I got it from his desk when Sims wasn't looking,' said Frank, producing a piece of chalk from his pocket. 'I'm going to write something on a tree or something. Just to show them. What do you think?'

'Mill's right,' said Les. 'You do, you want your head read.'

The dog appeared first, trotting along beside the hedge. But his handler and the other soldier weren't far behind.

The boys threw themselves to the ground. 'Blimey! Think they spotted us?' said Les.

'They can't. Not this far away.'

But suddenly the dog began to bark and with the soldiers in pursuit all three began to run towards the woods.

Frank grabbed his friend and hauled him to his feet. 'Leg it, Les! Quick!'

They crashed back through the trees, briars and branches catching at their legs and arms as they ran. At the foot of the wall Frank hoisted Les up and then scrambled after him. They dropped down on the other side and ran across the road for the safety of the fields beyond. But as they reached the top of the bank several figures stepped from the shadow of the barn and barred their way. It was George Poole, Wally Carr, and the rest of his gang.

'Well, now—what we got here, eh, lads?' said Poole.

'Don't mess about, Poole,' said Frank desperately. 'Just get out the way.'

But Poole and the rest didn't move. 'Why? What you been up to, then?' he said.

'Nothing. Just get out the way.' Their pursuers could not be far behind now and Frank and Les knew it. Once they looked over the wall they would recognize the two boys at once. Frank stepped forward but George Poole placed a hand on his chest.

'You ain't answered yet,' he said.

'Nothing. We haven't been doing anything.'

'Yes, you have,' said Wally Carr, the policeman's son. 'We seen you and him going over that wall.'

'That's right. And I reckon we knows what you been up to,' said Poole. 'Specially since you got your little pal with you.'

'We weren't doing anything.'

'Yes, you was. Tell them what they was doing, Wal.'

Wally Carr grinned. 'Stands to reason. You been poaching.'

Frank stared at him. 'Poaching?'

'Yes. 'Cos that's what gyppos and their pals do. Ain't it, Gill? Eh? You tell us what the gyppos do, gyppo.'

'I ain't a gyppo,' said Les.

'Don't say anything,' said Frank. 'He ain't a gypsy. He's a cockney.'

'Ain't a gyppo?' said George Poole, and laughed. ''Course he is. He sounds like a gyppo. And he looks like a gyppo.' Poole grinned at the rest of them. 'And what's more . . . ' He began to snigger. 'And what's more, them's gyppo trousers if ever I saw them!'

They were the ones Les always wore: the baggy corduroys Vera Thrale had made for him from an old pair of her husband's to replace the rags Les had arrived in. It hadn't occurred to her that he would be the only boy his age in the village with long trousers.

'So,' spluttered Poole, 'so if he sounds like a gyppo and looks like a gyppo and he's got gyppo trousers on, then I reckon that's what he is: he's Gyppo Gill!' And they all started to laugh.

'How come they didn't take you, then—Gyppo Gill?' asked Wally Carr. 'You know, when they took the rest of 'em away?'

'P'raps the Jerries will come back for him,' said Poole.

Frank launched himself at him and they fell to the ground. The rest caught hold of Les and held him while they formed a circle shouting encouragement. But the fight didn't last long. From nowhere it seemed two large hands reached down, grabbed the combatants by the scruff of the neck, and hauled them to their feet. Struggling, Frank and George Poole found themselves looking up at a red-faced young man with sandy-coloured hair.

'What's all this about, then?' he asked.

'You let go of me,' said Poole. 'You let go, d'you hear? I'm going to sort him out good and proper.'

'No, I can't have that,' said the young man, and grinned. 'Don't hardly seem fair, not with these odds.'

'Mind your own business! You ain't even from round here,' said Wally. 'My dad's a policeman. I shall tell him what you done.'

'Right you are, then,' said the young man. 'You tell him to pop over to Middelbury and have a word with me when he's got a minute. Naylor's the name; Ted Naylor. And I'll tell him how there was six of you laying into two of them. No—tell you what, you nip home now and fetch him out. Go on. I'll wait here for him.'

Poole rubbed his sleeve across his nose which was starting to bleed. 'Come on, Wal,' he said. 'Come on, you lot. You'll keep, Tate. And you, Gyppo.' And Wally Carr and the rest followed him away along the road.

'If I was you,' said the young man, 'I'd hop it, quick. In the other direction.'

'Thanks,' said Frank.

'No point going looking for trouble, is there? Not this side of the wall nor the other,' he added. 'Know what I mean?'

Frank and Les nodded.

'That's right. Off you go, then.'

They hurried away from the barn and climbed the gate into the field beyond. They looked back when they reached the other side but the young man was nowhere to be seen.

'Where did he come from, Les?'

'I don't know. But he saved our bacon and that's a fact.'

'And what happened to the Jerry guards and that dog? I thought they were right behind us.'

'P'raps it wasn't us they was after. Come on, Frank, let's get home.'

Chapter 3

The soldier they called 'Bumpsadaisy' swallowed the last of his beer, and calling to his companions, who were playing dominoes over by the fire, ordered them another round. When they'd closed up the checkpoint for the day the three Germans often went into The Shevington Arms for a drink. One or two of landlord Harry Poole's regulars took exception to them—Jack Cowdrey, who'd lost both his younger brothers during the Folkestone Landings, had been known to get up and walk out when they came in—but for the most part, the soldiers were tolerated even if it was grudgingly.

However, there was a particular tension in the air that evening. The announcement of the Hitler Birthday Celebrations only a few days before was still the subject of heated conversation in the bar at the 'Shevvy' and the Germans' welcome was distinctly cooler than usual. It was especially unfortunate that their presence coincided with one of Mr Underwood's occasional visits to the pub.

'I could ask 'em to leave, Mr Underwood,' Harry Poole suggested, when he served the headmaster his half-pint. 'That's if you really wanted me to.'

George Underwood shook his head; he knew Harry Poole too well. 'No, Harry,' he said. 'I wouldn't ask you to do that.'

It was a recent habit of the headmaster's, calling in at The Shevington Arms while he was out walking his dog last thing of an evening. He had come to realize that however normal things appeared on the surface people were still in a state of shock and that anxiety and uncertainty were never far away. How could it be otherwise, when all certainty had been overturned in those terrible days of autumn 1940? It was as though people had been winded, had had the life knocked out of them. It was the only way he could explain the terrible business with Cec Warwick and his family. It was months ago now, not long after the Germans arrived, but he knew the memory of it still rankled, still made people uncomfortable. The whole family bundled into a lorry and taken off. Shevington people wouldn't have just stood by and seen that happen—not before the war. But people weren't sure any more who or what they were. Even the children. He'd seen it in the silly arguments—even sillier than usual—which could suddenly turn the playground outside his window into a screaming, brawling, scrimmage; or in the way rumours, no matter how outlandish—the more outlandish, it seemed, the more powerful they were— could seize their imaginations at a moment's notice. And their fathers and mothers were no less vulnerable. So, he popped in to the 'Shevvy' once or twice a week towards nine-thirty. In case things began to slip, he told himself; to keep an eye on things. And as for the three Germans, George Underwood's anger was too deep to stop at a few noisy boys, who looked as though they should be behind a plough, not goose-stepping on other people's doorsteps.

'Another half, Mr Underwood?' said Harry Poole, giving the table top a wipe with his cloth. 'Go on, sir. On the house.'

'Thank you, no. I must be on my way.'

'But you've only had the one.'

'Quite sufficient, thank you. Bess?' Beneath the table the old labrador struggled to her feet and waddled to the door.

' 'Course, there's one or two took this Hitler business very hard,' said Harry confidentially, as the headmaster

rose. 'You know, all this celebrating and such. I
don't s'pose you know what it's going to entail, Mr
Underwood?'

'I'm afraid not. But I daresay Warden Firth will have
the details.'

'Only I was wondering if there would be any
arrangement made to provide an extra barrel, on the
day, as it were. I don't s'pose you've heard anything
about that?'

'We shall all hear in good time, Harry. That's one
thing of which you can always be sure—they're very
good at letting us know right away exactly what they
want us to do. Goodnight. Goodnight, everyone.'

'Goodnight, headmaster,' they chorused.

Mr Underwood and Bess crossed The Green and
turned for home. As they were passing the Scouts' hut,
Frank's Aunt Edie and her son Colin were coming out.
Edie had a brown paper parcel under her arm.

'Goodnight, Mr Underwood,' she said.

'Goodnight, Edith. Goodnight, Colin,' he replied.
'Edith?'

'Yes, Mr Underwood?'

'Is there any more news of your husband? Len, isn't
it?'

'Thank you for asking, Mr Underwood. Yes, he wrote
a month and more ago. We're expecting another letter
soon.'

'That must be a great solace to you.'

'Oh, yes, it is, sir.'

'Well, goodnight again.'

Edie and Colin hurried on. 'Wasn't that nice of him,'
she said, 'to ask like that. I always liked Mr Underwood.
He's a hero, you know, Colin?'

'Is he, ma?' said Colin. Though what interested him
more was the fact that his mother had called the
headmaster, 'sir'.

'Oh, yes. In the Great War. He got a medal. He was
wounded when Captain Elliott was killed at the Battle of

the Somme. Captain Elliott's sisters live out at Myrtle Lodge, where that teacher of yours stays: Mr Sims, isn't it?'

'The Toff.'

'What did you say?'

'I mean, that's what some of them call him.'

'Come on, put your best foot forward, it's time you were home in bed.'

'I've never seen Mr Underwood with a medal, ma.'

'No,' said Edie. 'Come to think of it, I don't think I have either.'

Frank was already asleep when Colin got upstairs; at least, his eyes were closed and he looked as though he was asleep.

The room they shared was small; the beds, pushed against opposite walls, took up most of the space. Between them was a small chest of drawers. The top of the chest of drawers was divided equally with a line of white chalk. Colin had drawn it there the day after Frank arrived. He had drawn it scrupulously; he wanted everything to be fair, he'd told Frank gravely; and had renewed it when necessary ever since. *The Scouting Manual*, the newly revised edition; a dog-eared Great Western Railway Timetable; six lead soldiers in red tunics and black busbies; and Colin's five-stones, were all arranged neatly on his side of the line, together with his encyclopaedia, the one that no one else was allowed to look at.

Frank's side was bare by comparison. The day the Germans came to The White Horse Inn he had had time only to bundle a few clothes into his case and to scoop what he could from the mantelpiece. Two photographs: one of him and his dad taken on the front at Seabourne—he was wearing his dad's hat in that one; and the other one of just his dad, leaning on the railings not far from the pier, hands in the pockets of his old flannel trousers and looking serious; those photos and the strip of metal with his name, age, and SEABOURNE

39

SUSSEX ENGLAND stamped into it—he'd made that in the Amusement Arcade, turning the heavy pointer to each letter in turn and then banging down the handle hard. That was all. Even if the soldier on the landing hadn't been shouting at him to hurry there wasn't much else he could have salvaged. Frank and his dad had always travelled light.

'Frank? . . . You awake, Frank? . . . Frank?'

'What?'

Colin turned on his side to look at him. 'I thought you were,' he said.

'What about it?'

'Frank, you know when you dream?' Frank didn't reply. 'I wish I could dream like that.'

'Like what?'

'Dream like you do.'

'What do you want to dream for?'

'I try to; I try hard.' Colin hesitated. 'I try to dream about my dad,' he said, 'but it doesn't work.'

''Course it doesn't,' said Frank. 'Dreams aren't like that.'

'No, I know. Frank?'

'What?'

'What was he like?'

'Who?'

'Your dad? When you first came, remember?' said Colin. 'You said he used to make you laugh. You told me that.'

'He did.'

'Did he? What did he do? Tell you jokes? Was it like Arthur Askey?'

Frank shook his head. 'No,' he said, 'he didn't tell jokes.'

'How did he make you laugh, then?'

Frank shrugged. 'He just did. We used to laugh at all sorts of things.'

'Was that when you lived at the seaside?'

'We lived in lots of places.'

40

'He wasn't in the army, was he?'

'He didn't have to be. They sent him to different factories instead.'

'Was that when you were small?'

'I don't know.' He couldn't remember; he thought he remembered living in one place for a time . . . his mother must have been with them then . . . but it was too long ago.

'Our dad used to take us to the park,' said Colin, 'me and Rose and our ma. And he took us to the pictures. That was when we lived in Swindon.'

'Go to sleep, Col.'

Somewhere on the other side of the village a dog began to bark and was answered by another. Then everything was quiet again. Frank lay staring at the ceiling. Wondering. Wondering if going over the wall into the grounds of Shevington Hall had been such a good idea. No—it had been a stupid idea. All it had proved was that it was hopeless trying. Even trying! Trying had just made him feel even more helpless. Perhaps . . . perhaps there really wasn't anything they could do . . . a couple of kids . . . on their own. Nothing at all.

'Frank?'

'What?'

'You know up at the Hall?'

'What about it?'

'I was wondering, that's all. I mean, do you think . . . Frank, do you think Rose talks to them?'

'Talks to who?'

'Only that's what Wally Carr said. At Scouts tonight.'

Frank turned to look at his cousin. 'Said what?' he said.

'He said that's what George Poole said. George said worse than that.' Colin's face blushed with embarrassment.

'What did he say? Colin?'

'He said there's some of 'em up at the Hall go . . . he said they go courting with Jerries.'

41

'He's a liar!' said Frank angrily. 'Did he say Rose goes courting with 'em?'

'No. He just said . . . you know.'

'If he says that about your sister Rose you tell him he's a liar.'

'All right.'

Frank turned away.

'Frank? When our dad comes home . . . '

'Go to sleep, Col.'

'Do you think we'll have to go back there?'

'Back where?'

'Back to Swindon?'

' 'Course you will.'

'That's what I thought. Goodnight, Frank. Frank?'

'What?'

'Goodnight.'

'Goodnight, Col.'

There had been a fire-beacon on the Downs above Middelbury in the days of the Armada; it had given its name to the narrow lane which climbed steeply from the village to the crest above. In more recent times the site had been occupied by an anti-aircraft battery; but its concrete emplacement and the pill-box nearby had been reduced to rubble by a Wehrmacht Demolition Unit not long after Christmas 1940.

It was a still, moonless night with a few ragged clouds motionless in the sky. The Curfew Patrol had almost reached the top of the lane, and the soldiers sitting either side of the open-topped lorry were looking forward to the soup that would be waiting for them at the barracks on the other side of the hill. Not far from the crest the road dipped through a deep hollow of ancient beech trees. The soldiers were laughing as they approached the hollow; the corporal had been explaining to them that a thousand and more years before, the ridges they were bumping over had been the ramparts of a mighty fortification to which the local inhabitants had retreated in times of danger. It was the sort of thing the corporal always knew; he had been a student before the war. They were laughing when the grenade dropped at their feet. They watched it as it tumbled along the floor and disappeared under the seat. The corporal took its full blast, which tore away the tailboard and sent the lorry careering off the road and into the gorse where it overturned and came to rest against a chalk outcrop.

The driver crawled from the cab and scrambled to his feet sweeping the darkness desperately with his torch. Its beam found them one by one scattered across the turf and road. The corporal was unquestionably dead; the others he bandaged, and comforted as best he could, before running back down the hill for help.

Someone stumbled on the stairs outside and a floorboard creaked. For a moment, as his eyes opened, Frank was uncertain where he was. The dream had been so vivid: his dreams always were. He had been back in the room at The White Horse Inn, the heavy curtains drawn against the daylight, the photographs on the walls, the table piled with tins of food, listening to that song Mr Burford always sang about the lilacs.

He listened as a door closed quietly further along the landing. Rose: it would be his cousin Rose coming in late. And out in the lane? Was that a motorbike pulling away? Or it might have just been a patrol going past. The trouble was once someone said something like the thing Colin said George Poole had said you started looking out for things, suspecting things. Could Rose really be courting with a Jerry? Perhaps 'that' was what her and Edie were always rowing about. But then, Edie was always rowing with somebody. She never seemed happy unless she was. It was just like his dad used to say: 'Our Edie's got a quick tongue, Frank. Her and me don't get along. It's

43

a long story. Harsh words and such on both sides. Bit late to kiss and make up.'

He was wide awake now. He got up quietly, pulled his jumper over his pyjamas, and went downstairs.

She was sitting in the dark in front of the range as he opened the kitchen door.

'Who's that?' she asked.

'Me, Nan. Sorry, Nan.'

'That's all right.'

'I was thirsty. I came for a drink of water.'

'Come in, then. There's a draught with that door open.'

He took a cup from the dresser and filled it at the tap. He felt awkward, finding her there like that, in the dark. You never knew with Nan which way she'd take a thing. He gulped down the cold, metallic water and started back towards the door.

'Been dreaming, have you?' she asked, without looking up from the dull glow in the grate.

'Me, Nan?'

'Have you?'

'Yes,' he said. And then: 'I can't help it.' She didn't answer, and he hesitated uncertainly in the doorway. 'Goodnight, Nan.'

'D'you want to sit for a minute?'

'I wouldn't mind.'

'Get yourself a chair then.'

He pulled a chair across to the fire and sat down opposite her. They sat like that for some time, both gazing into the glowing embers. Finally Nan said, 'Dream about your dad, do you?'

Frank shook his head. 'But I think about him,' he said. It was easy to say it there in the dark. 'It's afterwards I mostly dream about.'

'Afterwards?'

'After they'd come; the things that happened after the Germans came.'

'You did your best, Frank. You're only a boy.'

He looked sideways at her. She'd said it quietly without reproach. 'I went out looking, Nan,' he said. 'I tried to find him.'

The first time, the day when he'd climbed out through the coal-hole, when he'd tried to get to Bell's Precision where his dad was fire-watching, that day the streets had been impassable, filled with German soldiers who'd shouted at him and pointed their rifles. The next day he'd tried again and got as far as the Ivanhoe Hotel. The Ivanhoe was the only building on the seafront at Seabourne which had been badly damaged. Through its gaping door he could see the blackened walls and fallen ceilings. The VACANCIES sign still hung in one of the empty windows. And the day after that he'd reached the High Street, but it had been sealed off while long columns of lorries and men came ashore from down by the pier. So he'd gone back to The White Horse Inn. And waited. Just like Burford said he should.

'What would be the point of going out again, Frank? D'you see what I mean?'

They were in Burford's drawing room at the back of the house; the one with the piano and vase of paper flowers and all the photographs. And the big picture of the man who wrote the song about the lilacs: Ivor Novello he was called. The curtains were drawn, and Mr Burford was sharpening a wooden gramophone needle on the abrasive pad next to the baize-covered turntable.

'But there's bound to be a list or something, Mr Burford. Won't there be a list of who's wounded and who's—'

'What if there is, Frank? What sort of confidence can you have in a thing like a list? I know that from bitter experience. Don't I just! I had a dear friend, Frank, a chap with whom I'd corresponded for years and years. He lived in London; the New Cross area, where the bombing was so bad. That man's home was reduced to ashes, Frank, ashes and rubble. They put my friend on a list. Oh, yes. They even informed his sister in Woolwich that he was dead. And not three days later that man walked into the ARP Station as alive as you or me. He hadn't been home that night, you see? He hadn't been there. See what I mean? I can show you the letter he sent me. Oh, we did laugh. You hear stories like that all the time, Frank. Them and their lists! You eat up and don't go worrying your head about lists.'

Slices of peach in a thick, cloying syrup. Burford had tins of them. His table was piled with boxes and tins that he'd laid by.

'Dad'll come home,' he said, fitting the needle into the arm of the gramophone. 'Nothing surer, Frank. And when he does, this is where he'll want to find you. Oh, Frank, just think if he was to come running up those steps out there and you weren't here? What if you were out looking for lists? What if you'd got yourself into hot water somewhere? There are terrible things happening out there, Frank. I know what your dad would want, he'd want you to wait here for him safe and sound.'

'I want to be here when he comes, Mr Burford.'

''Course you do! And that's what we've got to do, Frank, wait. You and me, eh? We'll wait together.'

Burford cranked the handle and began to lower the needle carefully on to the turning record.

'But, Mr Burford, what if—'

'Ssshh!' Burford raised a finger to his lips. 'Just listen to the music, Frank. It's a lovely song. Mother and I never missed one of Ivor's shows, you know. No—not ever. We used to go up on the early train. Shall we sing it together?'

'I don't know the words, Mr Burford.'

''Course, you do. You sing it with me, eh, Frank? You've got a lovely young voice:

'"We'll gather lilacs in the spring again,
And walk together down an English lane;
Until our hearts have learned to sing again,
When you come home once more."'

46

He did know the words. Lilacs and spring and everything being all right again. He'd heard them often enough as Burford's gramophone played them. Over and over. But he didn't join in.

It was true: it made sense to wait. So he waited and watched from the big bay window. Weary groups of refugees with prams piled with suitcases and mattresses; small children and old men and women struggling after them. The sea busy all day long, landing-craft and motorboats hurrying between the shore and the warships anchored on the horizon. One afternoon a military band went past playing cheerful music. He sat there day after day waiting for his dad to appear striding along the Promenade. But he never came.

In the end it was the Germans who came. Early one morning. They came to requisition the house. Frank ran upstairs at once and bundled what he could into a suitcase. The last thing he remembered seeing in the room he and his dad had shared all those months were his dad's best shoes neatly aligned beside the bed. Then the soldier ordered him outside.

He walked all that day and most of the next. The roads were crammed with endless, slow-moving columns of people. And soldiers in lorries with 'To London!' chalked along their sides. He spent the night in a roofless barn with a man and woman who said they were from Brighton. And next morning he took the road over the Downs and descended into the winding, silent lanes on the other side. It took the rest of the day to find Shevington and the small, delapidated cottage where his grandmother lived.

Even there he'd gone on waiting. He'd gone every day to stand at the gate expecting to see . . . no, expecting wasn't the word, it sounded too sure, too certain, and it hadn't been like that; it was more that for a long time he wouldn't have been at all surprised to see his dad coming up the lane. To see him wave and call out: 'Hello, old son! I thought I'd find you here. Sorry it took so long but the place is crawling with Jerries.' And hear him laugh. But he never came. And he wouldn't—not now. That was the hardest part to get used to: that he wouldn't come. That he would never come home again.

He looked up from the firelight and found Nan watching him.

'You've got too much to remember, Frank,' she said. 'That's why you dream.'

'Do you dream, Nan?' he asked.

'Now and then.'

'Is that why you can't sleep at night?'

'I don't need sleep same as you, Frank. Besides, I like sitting here in the quiet.'

'Do you think about my dad sometimes, Nan?'

'I do.'

They were silent again for a while. Then:

'That was always the first thing he did, Nan: send a postcard to tell you where we were. From all the places they sent him to. They kept sending him to different factories, you see. Miles away.'

'He was t'other side of the Downs, Frank.'

Frank looked across at her but she remained gazing steadily into the last of the fire. It was true. They had been twenty miles away—less. When his dad was first transferred to Seabourne, not long after Dunkirk, he'd looked Shevington up on the map, twisting the metal tape-measure this way and that, measuring the distance as precisely as possible. And not long after he'd seen the name Shevington on the front of one of the buses that stopped up at the Circus. He'd told his dad so. But his dad had said: 'I know, son. But not presently, eh? Not with Edie there. I explained that to you, didn't I? But there's something you must promise me, old son. If ever there should be a need that's where you must go. I want you to promise me that, Frank. All right?'

'A bus-ride from home and he never came.'

'But he couldn't, Nan.'

48

'Why not?'

'Because Edie was here.'

'What's that got to do with it?'

Frank shrugged. 'Because she hated him. He told me.'

'Is that what he said?' Frank nodded. 'Put a shovelful of slack on the fire for me,' said Nan; 'we might keep it in a bit longer.' He filled the shovel from the scuttle and sprinkled the dusty coal over the dying embers. When he sat down again she said, 'D'you remember your mother at all, Frank?'

'No.'

'No—no, I don't s'pose you would; you were too young. She led your poor father a dance, Frank. I won't say any more than that. And Edie couldn't forgive her for that; that and leaving you both the way she did. But the thing she couldn't forgive more than anything was the fact that your dad wouldn't hate the woman for what she done; she couldn't forgive him for that.'

'He didn't hate her.'

'Why d'you say that?'

'He had a picture of her. It was in his wallet.'

'A picture of who?'

'My mother.'

'Ah, Bill,' she sighed, 'you fool.' Her gaze returned to the darkened grate. 'You better get along back to bed, Frank,' she said finally. 'Go on.'

'Goodnight, Nan,' he said. But she didn't answer. 'Nan?'

'What is it?'

'I had a go at Warden Firth the other evening.'

'Edie told me.'

'I ain't sorry, Nan.'

'I never thought you would be.'

'It's all wrong, Nan. We ought to be paying them back, not doing what they tell us to. Why doesn't somebody pay them back?'

'We just have to go on hoping as one day somebody will.'

49

'That's what I hope all the time.'

'Consider Garibaldi, Frank.'

'Yes, Nan.' He thought about asking her why the picture had suddenly gone from the kitchen wall. 'Nan?'

'What's that?'

'Nothing.'

'Long as we hope, Frank, then they ain't got us beat. You remember that. Goodnight.'

'Goodnight, Nan.'

Chapter 4

She caught up with him not far from the end of the lane.

'Frank?' she called. And he turned and waited for her.

'Hello, Rose.'

'Mind if I walk along with you?' she said.

''Course not.'

He glanced sideways at her as they walked. She was wearing her headscarf like a turban with her blonde hair tucked up inside it. Just like the film stars in those old *Picturegoer* magazines she was always looking at. Seventeen she was. But she looked older. She didn't have lipstick on; she wasn't allowed lipstick when she was working. But she was wearing scent. Californian Poppy, it would be. She'd told him once before that that was her favourite.

'I'm early this morning,' she said. 'But I'm on evenings these next two weeks. Pity, really. I'm going to miss the Film Show. They're due again, aren't they?'

'You won't miss much,' he said.

'Oh, Frank,' she laughed, 'don't be such an old misery.'

'It's only the Jerries marching everywhere. Or factories. Or people singing. Who wants to watch that?'

'Oh, I know it's not proper pictures,' she said. 'I mean, it's not Robert Taylor and Greta Garbo. Did you ever see *Camille*, Frank? That's my favourite. I mean, I know it's not like that. But it's better than nothing.'

There was hardly anyone at the checkpoint on The Green and 'Bumpsadaisy' let Frank through without looking at his Identity Card. But he stopped Rose. He

51

smiled, and stood comparing the photograph on her card with the young woman in front of him.

'*Schöne,*' he said.

'Thank you, kind sir,' she said, and dropped the card back in her bag. '*Auf Wiedersehn.*'

'What did you say to him?' Frank asked as they walked away.

'T.T.F.N. You know, ta-ta for now.'

'What was that he said to you first?'

Rose smiled. 'Beautiful,' she said. 'That's the way they say it. Nice, en't it?'

'D'you talk to them a lot, Rose?'

'Well, you have to, Frank. Up at the Hall. I mean, they often speak to me. Perfect English, too. Just like toffs. And they've got lovely manners. They're ever so polite. They are, Frank.'

Frank shrugged.

'They are. Honest. Some of them are really nice.'

'That's the bell,' he said, looking across towards the school gates. 'I've got to go. Cheerio, Rose.'

'*Wiedersehn,*' she called.

Frank didn't approve, Rose could tell. Some people didn't. Nan didn't. She hadn't, not from the first. Not even when Sir Quentin had still been up at the Hall. And when the General had taken over Nan had been really rude about a granddaughter of hers working there. Thankfully, for a change, her mother had been on her side and she'd told Nan flat that they needed the money. And they had, what with Frank arriving out of the blue not long after. Besides, it would have taken more than Nan's disapproval to make Rose stop working at the Hall—she loved it too much.

And to think how she'd cried herself sick at having to leave Swindon. When the news came that her father had been captured at Dunkirk her mother had immediately packed their bags and got them all on to a bus to Shevington. 'There won't be no stopping the Germans now,' she'd said. 'We'll be safer in the country.' Rose had been inconsolable at having to leave her friends. Oh, but if those friends could see her now! Shevington Hall! A by-word for gracious living, Rose. That's what Mrs Swinburne, the housekeeper, called it. They've all been here, she'd told her: cabinet ministers, captains of industry, leading members of the theatrical profession. And the Duke of Windsor, the Prince of Wales as he was then, used to stay with Sir Quentin on a regular basis. Mrs Swinburne could remember the night the Duke played the banjo to them all out on the terrace. The housekeeper had told her that in an unguarded moment and had made her swear never to reveal it to a living soul.

Shevington Hall! Even now, after so many months, it was still like a dream. Or a film. It was like being in a film. Rose wouldn't have been at all surprised to meet Sir Cedric Hardwicke on the stairs. Or, even nicer, Robert Taylor.

'*Ich nehme ihn!*'

'*Nein, zu mir!*'

On the tennis court at the back of the house four young men in white shirts and trousers were calling to each other as they sent the ball to and fro.

'*Ausgezeichnet! Ausgezeichnet!*'

Suddenly the two of them ran forward and jumped over the net. They stood shaking hands and laughing with their opponents. One of them had hair so fair it was almost white. He was the one everyone talked about. Honeyger his name was. Or something like that. 'Hard as nails' they all said he was. He didn't look it. Actually he looked quite nice. Besides, Rose couldn't see how anyone with hair like that could be a secret policeman. One of the others looked up to where she was standing and waved and said something she couldn't quite catch. Rose blushed, and hurried away down the steps to the servants' hall.

No one had expected Peter Sims to stay in Shevington. It was meant to be a temporary arrangement until Mr

Underwood's son, Henry, came home from the war and resumed his post. But Henry Underwood hadn't come home; he had been killed in one of the great tank battles which had rolled backwards and forwards across the Midlands in the desperate days before the Surrender. And Peter Sims had stayed. 'Although, to be perfectly honest, I'm not sure I'm cut out for teaching at all,' he'd told Mr Underwood. 'But it is such an important role in times as desperate as these.' Mr Underwood had nodded his agreement—on both scores.

Mr Sims unrolled the map and hooked it over the top of the blackboard.

ROME AND ITS EMPIRE, it read.

Then he turned and faced them. That was the moment he always found most daunting. But he had prepared this lesson well. After all, it was his subject.

'Thank you? Thank you?' The chattering dropped to a low whisper. 'At its height,' he began, 'at its height the Roman Empire encompassed most of Europe, the Middle East, and North Africa. The *Pax Romana* purported to bring with it the civilizing advantages of a unanimity which was both—'

'What's them lines, sir?'

'The lines?'

'On the map, sir?'

'Ah, those lines. Yes, I suppose they are the first things one actually notices. They are roads, Libby, Roman roads. Can you all see them?'

There were one or two murmurs of confirmation.

'Can you imagine, there was a time when you could walk from Carlisle to the furthest wilds of Asia Minor along Roman roads? Just look at them. An extraordinary feat of engineering. How straight they are! Straight as arrows shot from the Roman bow. Straight to the heart of her conquests. Quite relentless. That is how you recognize a Roman road, it never seems to have any doubt about where it's going or stops to change its mind.' Peter Sims laughed nervously. 'If you see what I mean?'

'Like the Nazis,' said Frank.

'What do you mean, Tate?'

'Like the Nazis. They build roads everywhere, don't they?'

'You'm a right crackpot, Tate,' said George Poole. 'The Romans wasn't Nazis, was they, Mr Sims?'

'Not . . . not in our meaning of the word. The Romans . . . ' Sims seemed flustered. 'After all,' he said, 'the Romans flourished two thousand years and more before the . . . the . . . the Nazis and—'

'But they build roads,' insisted Frank. 'That's the same. I've seen them on the newsreels. That's what the Nazis do wherever they go.'

'Quite so,' said Sims. 'Is there . . . is there anything else we know about the Romans?'

'They lived over Patfield way, sir,' said Marge Prout.

'Who did?'

'They had a house not far from the cottage hospital.'

'Ah! You mean the palace! Of course. Yes, so they did. Quite correct, Margery,' said Sims. 'I shouldn't have forgotten that, should I? Patfield Palace is one of the jewels of our Romano-British inheritance.'

'It ain't a palace,' said George Poole.

'I been past it hundreds of times,' said Wally Carr, 'and I ain't never seen no palace.'

'It's just a few old stones in a field.'

'Of course it is,' said Sims enthusiastically. 'I mean,' he scooped at his hair eagerly, 'that's just the point, don't you see? It is just a pile of stones. *Sic transit gloria mundi!*'

'How d'you mean, sir?' said several voices.

There was a knock at the classroom door and Miss Meacher came in. She had been standing outside for some minutes listening and wondering whether to interrupt. Romans! Poor Mr Sims, with his college ways—Cambridge, no less. It was a mystery he'd come to somewhere like Shevington in the first place. He meant well; he always did. But the sooner he was

55

informed the better. These Ministry men were under strict orders—these days who wasn't under strict orders?—to sort the wheat from the chaff. The more time he had to prepare himself, the more chance there would be for him to make a good impression.

'Do excuse me, Mr Sims,' she said.

'Miss Meacher? We . . . we were just discussing the . . . um . . . the Romans.'

'Yes. I'm sorry to interrupt, but I thought it best that we all knew as soon as possible: the headmaster has just received a phone call from the Ministry, we are to expect a visit from a Schools Inspector sometime in the next couple of days.'

'A Schools Inspector?'

'Yes.' And Miss Meacher almost added: I'm afraid so; but stopped herself in time. 'It is most inconsiderate to give us such short notice; and quite unexpected.'

'He is coming to inspect us?'

'Yes, Mr Sims.' The man really was impossible. 'He is an Inspector, Mr Sims; a Mr Forbes-Handley.'

'Oh, good Lord!' The colour drained from Peter Sims's face and he began to rake his hair between his fingers.

'Mr Sims, are you all right?'

Sims sat down at the desk. 'Yes . . . yes,' he said. 'It is something of a shock, that's all.'

'Yes. But forewarned is forearmed, don't you think?'

'I suppose it is, yes. Thank you, Miss Meacher. Most considerate.'

'I'll leave you to your Romans, then.'

'Thank you.'

When she'd gone Sims remained at the desk and seemed to have completely forgotten the lesson.

Someone laughed.

And Frank said, 'They salute the same as well, don't they? Sir?'

Sims looked up. 'Tate? What is it?'

'The Nazis' salute—it's the same as the Romans, isn't it? I've seen that at the pictures—in films.'

56

'Very similar, Tate.' Sims got up suddenly. 'I'd . . . I'd like you all to copy the map into your books,' he said.

'But, sir.'

'Just do it!' And he turned away and went over to stand at the window.

'It was just getting interesting and all,' said Frank. 'Useless!'

But the teacher didn't seem to hear.

The photograph on Mr Underwood's desk always made Miss Meacher feel uncomfortable. Three young men in army uniforms standing in front of a tank. The one in the middle was so like his father it might have been the headmaster himself standing there. She found it slightly eerie. And terribly sad. Poor Mr Underwood. People said that in normal times Henry Underwood would have been awarded a medal. Like his father. By which they meant, of course, if Britain had won and not the other way round. There were no heroes in a defeated army.

'You say he took it badly? Miss Meacher?'

'I'm so sorry, headmaster? I was miles away.'

'You were saying that Mr Sims took the news badly?'

'Yes, yes, he went very pale.'

'If we lose him, we'll find it very hard to maintain any sort of curriculum. Replacements are like gold dust, as you know. And a school the size of ours has no priority whatsoever.'

'No, headmaster. Which does make it seem all the more odd, does it not?'

'Odd?'

'That they should choose a school the size of ours for such an unexpected inspection.'

'Blitzkrieg, Miss Meacher. It is the Hitlerian method in all things.'

'But he is English, surely—this Mr Forbes-Handley?'

'He will have a job to do, none the less. Now, I wonder what that's all about.' Mr Underwood indicated the playground beyond the window where what looked like the entire school was crowded into the area next to the tap. 'Can the inspector's visit already have seized the popular imagination?'

'That or some other silliness,' sighed Miss Meacher. 'They believe every tittle-tattle and wild fancy that comes their way.'

'It seems to be young Poole who is the centre of attention.'

George Poole went home at dinnertimes and it was from the bar of the 'Shevvy' he had brought the news.

'It's a fact,' he told the crowd pressing around him; 'he's over there now in the snug. You go and see if you don't believe me.'

'When did it happen then, George?' asked Wally Carr.

'Two days ago. This chap was there the day after and he said you couldn't move for soldiers everywhere. Our dad knows him. He's a traveller for the disinfectant people. He wouldn't make it up.'

'Where did it happen?' asked Frank.

'Up on the road to Middelbury Beacon. In the dark. They killed a corporal and wounded two more of 'em with a hand-grenade.'

'Did they get away?'

'Yes. But he said there's a big search going on for 'em.'

Mr Underwood appeared on the steps and rang the bell for them to come back in. The crowd followed George Poole excitedly. Frank and Les walked slowly behind.

'What d'you think, Les?'

Les shrugged. 'You don't expect it round here, do you? In the wilds of Wales or somewhere but not here.'

'But somebody's fighting back, Les. That's the important thing!'

'It's probably just another of them daft rumours, that's all.'

'No,' said Frank implacably. 'That's just it, rumours

are always daft; that's how you know they're rumours. This ain't daft, Les.'

Colin had spread newspaper on the kitchen table and was busy cleaning his Scouts' belt; rubbing at it with a piece of rag, which he dampened from time to time from a bottle of Thawpit. He looked up to where his mother was sewing his new Scouts' shirt.

'Just the same mind, ma,' he said. 'I want all my badges back where they were. Mr Dearman says I'm the only one who appreciates the value of being well turned out. That's why he's chosen me to carry the flag at the celebrations. On The Day. Did you know that, Frank?'

'No,' said Frank. And wondered why when he wasn't sounding like a big kid his cousin invariably sounded like an old man. Outside the window the rain was falling heavily. Nan would surely be home soon. She couldn't stay out in this weather. And Nan would know. Nan knew things long before anyone else. Nan had her ear to the ground. If George Poole's story about Middelbury was true Nan would know. It had to be true. You couldn't dismiss something like that as just a rumour. Like Les had. Les just didn't want to believe it. He was funny like that. This wasn't a rumour; this was different. You had to believe something like this.

' "Smartness in one's turn-out is frequently indicative of a correct mental and political attitude," ' said Colin. 'It's all in the new manual, ma. I'm learning it off by heart. I shall want you to test me later.'

'I've got ironing to get on with,' she said. 'You get Frank to test you.'

'Hear that, Frank?'

Frank nodded.

'Mr Dearman was asking about you, Frank.'

'Me?'

'What was he asking?' said Edie, looking up from her needle.

'He asked why Frank never brought the forms back—for joining the troop.'

'You tell him that's because your cousin Frank never thinks of anybody but himself, that's why.'

'Nan said I didn't have to join if I didn't want to,' said Frank.

'Yes. And how do you think that makes Colin look, eh? Now then,' Edie held up her son's shirt. 'That good enough for you?'

'Oh, ma! I say!' Colin wiped his hands and took the shirt from her reverently. 'Oh, that is pie-hot, ma!' All his attainment badges were lined up along the sleeve; and on the collar she had neatly sewn the two discreet swastika roundels with which the troop had recently been issued. 'Smartest shirt on parade, I reckon. What do you think, Rose?' he asked, as his sister came in from the yard.

Rose shook the rain from her headscarf. 'Very smart, Col. Dib dib dib!'

'Go and hang it up, Colin,' said his mother. 'I won't have you teasing him, Rose, d'you hear? He's very proud of his Scouts.'

'I was only joking,' she said. 'Evening, Frank.'

''Lo, Rose.' It was difficult what with the sound of the rain and Colin chattering on the way he did, but Frank was pretty sure he hadn't heard any motorbike out in the lane. She had come home alone.

Rose took off her coat and hung it on the door. 'Know what? I could kill and maim for a cup of tea.'

'I'll make you one,' he said.

'You're a lover. Mother,' she said collapsing into the chair and pulling off her shoes, 'if I was to tell you the things I've seen today you'd go all of a heap!'

'That a fact?' Edie unfolded the ironing-board.

'Treasures, that's what. Priceless heirlooms they've had locked away for years and years. Mrs Swinburne said the last time they had them out was when the Duke of Windsor came to stay. Bone china dinner services; and you've never seen so many plates; and silver candlesticks and soup tureens. She's had us taking them out of their packing and cleaning them all day. I've been nervous as a cat for fear of dropping something, ma.'

'What's all that in aid of, then?'

'It's a secret. Nobody's s'posed to know. But there en't a lot gets past Joycie Prout. She heard Mr Jarvis, the butler, saying how there'll be people coming from miles around. And there's a plane coming from France with wines and food.'

'Who's coming, girl? Do talk sense.'

'The Nasty big-wigs. All the ones from the Southern Area Command and some others as well, that's what Joycie heard him say. They're coming to the Hall. They're having a banquet on old Hitler's birthday.'

'Here's your tea, Rose,' said Frank, and put the cup down on the table beside her.

'Thanks, lover. And know what else, mother?' There was a noise outside the back door and Rose turned and looked out of the window. 'Here's Nan,' she said.

The back door opened and Nan came in. She wore her sou'wester and oilskin cape from which the rain ran down onto the flagstones.

'Good God, mother,' said Edie, 'you're soaked.'

'No, I'm not,' she said. 'Evenin', Rose. Evenin', Frank.'

'Have you heard the news, Nan?' said Rose.

'What news is that?'

'It's supposed to be a secret but there's going to be a big do up at the Hall the night of old Hitler's birthday; they'll be coming from all over the county. And d'you know what? Joycie says they're bound to need extra staff to do the serving and everything. And they're bound to ask us. She says they'll give us a proper outfit to wear and everything. Just think of it, eh? I can see it now— all the candlelight and uniforms and gold and silver!'

'You're a dreamer, Rose Worth! That's what you are,' said Nan. 'It's just a lot of blessed Nazis guzzling theirselves silly. You shouldn't be having any truck with 'em. I don't s'pose anybody's seen to the hens, have they?' she said, and went back out into the rain.

'And where are you going?' said Edie, as Frank got up.

'To help Nan.'

She was down at the end of the run. There was a chicken balanced on her wrist as she scattered the scraps from the bowl and another perched on her sou'wester. 'See to the eggs for me, Frank,' she called.

He lifted the lid on the side of the coop and searching in the straw found four.

'Only four.'

She came across and took the eggs from him.

'Did you hear the news, Nan?' he said.

'What, that silly nonsense Rose was going on about?'

'No; what they did over Middelbury way.'

'I heard.'

'Is it true, Nan?' Nan looked at him and nodded. 'I knew it was!' he said. 'Nan! Somebody's fighting back at last. Who was it, Nan?'

'Nobody knows, Frank. Probably best they don't and all.'

'I wish I knew! I wish I knew, Nan, and I'd go and help them. I would!'

'Yes,' she said, 'I daresay you would. Come on, we better get on in. Or Edie'll cuss me for letting you get soaked through.'

Chapter 5

SS Hauptsturmführer Martin Honegger stood at the window of his office. The commanding view of the formal gardens at the back of Shevington Hall was one of the reasons he had chosen the room; their calm geometry had seemed an apt and reassuring reflection of the precision which the Hauptsturmführer valued so highly in his own life and work. He had transferred SS Administration to its present location as soon as he arrived at the Hall. The cramped quarters his predecessor had found satisfactory did not suit the young officer's requirements at all. But then, his predecessor had been easily satisfied: it was the reason he had been removed. The Hauptsturmführer needed space if he was to be effective. And to be effective he needed information. His records and filing-cabinets now lined the walls of the garden room on three sides from floor to ceiling.

There was a knock at the door and Oberleutnant Werner Lang, the General's secretary, came in.

'The General would like to see the arrangements for the operation in Middelbury this evening,' he said. 'Are they ready?'

'They are on the desk.'

Lang picked up the file.

'Did you think they would not be ready?' enquired Honegger casually.

'Not ready? Oh, no, Hauptsturmführer, certainly not.' Most certainly not. Whatever the Hauptsturmführer had anything to do with was always ready. On the dot. Not a blot or correction. That was the way the SS operated. The Oberleutnant had watched the Schutzstaffeln grow and grow, combining their Nazi Party politics and their security work with a grim and relentless precision. And they were everywhere now. What was it the General had said? 'There is one in every apple, Werner. Bite carefully.' The young officer glanced across at the figure by the window. It was a pity—the fellow played an excellent game of tennis. 'I will return the file as soon as the General has considered it,' he said.

'There will be no need.' Honegger turned from the window. 'I have copies.'

'Of course. Thank you, Hauptsturmführer.'

'*Heil Hitler.*'

'*Heil Hitler.*'

The sentry at the gates of Shevington Hall looked up and watched the old woman on the bicycle as she came slowly along the road. She passed by most days. But orders were orders. He stepped out into her path and held up his hand.

'*Bitte?*'

'What's all this in aid of?' asked Nan Tate, coming to a halt beside him.

'I must look at you,' said the soldier.

'What for?'

'Into your basket.'

'You've never done that before.'

'I must look.'

'Go on, then,' she said.

The soldier shouldered his rifle and began to search the basket hanging on the handlebars. Nan folded her arms and waited. It was never a good idea to let them see you were in a hurry.

Past the gates and the guard-house, half a mile away at the end of the curving gravel drive, the Hall rose proudly among its ancient woods and rolling parklands.

A broad flight of steps climbed to its columned portico, where, from the tall pillars either side of the entrance, two long, red banners hung, each with its white circle where the black swastikas clung like spiders.

And they'd have hung there a sight sooner, Nan reckoned, if Sir Quentin Demeger had had his way. Wicked old devil! Hadn't he had Germans to stay with him time and again before the war? Bold as brass. Driving about the countryside with their picnic baskets; and cameras. There were two of them stopped young Tom Gingell, the blacksmith's son—young Tom as was killed in one of the battles over in Wales—stopped him and asked him if he wanted to go back to Germany with them. Damned cheek!

'*Bitte?*'

'What's that?'

'You may go on,' said the sentry. 'Your basket is empty.'

Nan remounted and pedalled away. The cheek of it! Chits of boys telling folk whether they could come or go, where and when, stop and start, rooting about in people's bags. Just you wait, my lad—the day will come.

'The day will come!' That was what Pat used to say. 'Always consider Garibaldi.' The picture of Garibaldi and his other shirt was all her husband had had with him the summer he'd come tramping across the Downs. Was it so long ago? It seemed like yesterday he'd stopped by the gate. All the way from Ireland. Taking work where he could find it. Dear Pat who never gave up and wouldn't let anyone else give up either no matter how hard times were. And they were, through the years that followed the Great War—so hard. 'It'll come, Anne,' he'd say, and point to the red-shirted hero gazing steadfastly into the sun. 'Can't you see by the look of him he knows that it will! Sure, the hoping is all!'

About a mile further along the road Nan turned off on to a rutted track which brought her to a gate and farmyard. There was a collie dog sitting beside the gate, but he seemed to recognize her and made no sound as she opened it and walked through into the yard on the other side.

'Anybody home?' she called.

A man and a boy emerged from a nearby barn and came across to where she was standing.

'And how are you, Mrs Tate?' said the man. 'Haven't seen you for a day or two. Everything all right, I trust?'

'As well as can be expected, John Follett. And how are you, Ned?'

'He's very well, en't you, Ned?' said the man, turning to the boy. 'Pop in home, there's a good boy, and fetch out some of those potatoes for Mrs Tate.'

They watched him run inside.

'Is there any more news, John?'

John Follett nodded gravely. 'There is. There's another of them died; one of the Jerries who was wounded. They've sealed Middelbury right off near as dammit. They're in earnest and there's no knowing what nastiness they'll turn to. Capable of anything presently, I reckon.'

'People only got to remember what they done to Cec Warwick and his family.'

'It ain't forgot, Mrs Tate.'

'Now then, I've got some news for you,' said Nan. 'About this banquet they've got planned.'

'A banquet?'

'Up at the Hall. It'll be on the night of Hitler's birthday. They'll be coming from all over the Southern Area Command, John, and beyond; all the Nazi bigwigs. They'll all be there. I thought you ought to know.'

'I'm obliged to you, Mrs Tate.'

'Here's young Ned,' said Nan, as the boy came running from the house carrying some new potatoes in a bowl. 'I say, they do look fine!'

'Put them in Mrs Tate's basket, Ned.'

The boy frowned. 'What, all of 'em, Dad?'

'That's right.'

'That's very generous, John, thank you,' said Nan. 'Well, I'd better be on my way. Goodbye, Ned. And thank you again, John.'

'Thank you, Mrs Tate. Always welcome, you know that.'

As Nan cycled off down the track Ned Follett looked up at his father.

'What did you thank her for?' he said. 'She never brings us anything.'

'Just being neighbourly, Ned,' his father replied. 'They can't stop us being that.'

Was it the last of the green-tomato chutney?

Betty Firth climbed on to a chair and peered into the back of the cupboard. Yes, it was the last jar. And the plum preserve? There were only two jars of that left. And it had been such a wonderful crop. Well, she sighed, perhaps this year, things not being quite so frantic as last autumn, there would be time to do the fruit trees justice.

She reached down the chutney jar. Those young fellows from the Mobile Film Unit would appreciate something home-made. A cheese and chutney sandwich; and perhaps an egg and cress for the officer.

Betty had never really had much time for the cinema. It had always seemed a rather questionable pastime, sitting in a darkened building with a lot of people you didn't know. And the stories that filled the screen always seemed so exaggerated; so many desperate or rather shady types banging on, as her father would have said, about . . . well, about themselves really. Her visits to the cinema had been rare even during the brief time she had lived in London, which seemed to be full of them; and the nearest now was the Bioscope in Patfield and it certainly wasn't worth the trouble of going there and back. There had been occasional lantern shows in the village hall and they were often quite fun. But the

Mobile Film Unit was something quite different. The hour-long programmes they brought with them had impressed her; they were awfully well made and so informative.

Information. That was so important. In every way. It was one of the first things SS Hauptsturmführer Honegger had said to her when he took over at the Hall. 'Information is always the key, dear lady. Information . . . and fear. With those two at your disposal you can drain the last drop of hope from even the most resourceful opponent.' She had felt quite upset by the remark. But he had said it with such a boyish, mischievous smile that she was sure he must have been pulling her leg.

This evening would be the Unit's third visit. The first had been very well attended. Newsreels from all over Europe; and a delightful short film which followed two young soldiers around the sights of London. So fascinating to see the city through the eyes of strangers. And what memories it had brought back seeing it all again. The turn-out for the second visit hadn't been quite as good. This evening's programme, she decided, would require her to make some calls. The announcement she'd placed in Dearman's shop window couldn't be relied on to do the trick by itself. No, people would need reminding. She had a list somewhere of those who hadn't attended the last time. Now where had she put it?

Edie was usually what Nan called 'a tartar' when it came to staying at the table; but that evening she was up at the sink and gathering in the dirty plates before anyone had finished their tea.

'Colin?'

'Ma?'

'Upstairs soon as you're finished and change that shirt.'

'For heaven's sake, girl, leave him be!' said Nan. 'You'll have us all destroyed with heartburn or worse.'

'And what about you, Frank?'

'What?'

'What d'you mean, what? Aren't you going to tidy yourself up?'

'What for?' he asked. But he knew what was coming.

'You know very well what for, my lad. Colin!'

'I'm going. I am,' said Colin, and hurried upstairs.

'What about you, mother?'

'Just stop your fussing, Edie,' said Nan. 'I've only got to put me hat on. You go and sort yourself out.'

Frank waited until Edie had gone and then looked across the table at Nan. 'Nan?' he said. 'You ain't going, are you?'

'I am,' she said.

'But why?'

'And you're going with me.'

'We didn't go last time. Me and you didn't go. We stayed home.'

Nan didn't look up from her plate. 'Well,' she said, 'we're going tonight.'

'But why?'

'Betty Firth was round this afternoon, that's why.'

'We don't have to go because of her, do we?'

'I don't like it no more than you do but there's some things we has to do in spite. She's told Edie she'll hurry through the letter to your Uncle Len. And Edie wants us to keep her sweet for a while. It ain't a lot to ask.'

'Was that why you took Garibaldi down?'

''Course it was,' said Nan irritably. 'Now go and get ready while I look for me hat.'

'You coming as well?' asked Colin, as Frank came into the bedroom.

'What's it look like?'

'I only asked. Only you didn't, did you—last time?'

69

'No, I didn't. 'Cos I don't like wasting my time watching a lot of stupid Nazis marching and singing and telling us how clever they are.'

'You shouldn't go on like that, Frank,' said his cousin.

'I'll go on how I like.'

'I know. But in the end . . . '

'What, in the end?'

'I mean, in the end you have to give in. Like everybody else. Like tonight.'

'Look, I'm only coming so your dad can get his letters, see? That's all. And I don't even know your dad. I'm coming 'cos Nan says we have to keep that Firth sweet.'

Colin watched him as he took his jumper from the drawer and pulled it on. Then: 'I've been wondering about that,' he said. 'Frank?'

'What?'

'You know what you said the other day—do you still think we'll have to go back when he comes home? Will we have to go back to Swindon?'

''Course you will. That's where you live.'

'But that's what I mean, you see. I don't want to. I've got Scouts here. And Rose, she's got her job and everything. It's not . . . it's not fair.'

Frank looked across to where he sat on his bed.

'What's not fair?'

Colin looked down at the floor. 'You know—him,' he said quietly. 'Coming home and everything.'

'Your dad? Don't you want him to come home?'

'I don't know.'

'You must know, Col! He's your dad.'

'I know. But . . . it just doesn't seem fair.'

'Colin?' came the shout from the stairs. 'And you, Frank!'

Colin jumped up. 'Coming, ma. Frank,' he said, 'you won't tell anyone what I said, will you? You won't, will you?'

Frank shook his head. 'No,' he said.

70

'Colin!'

'Coming, ma.'

Colin hurried out and Frank followed him downstairs to where Edie and Nan were waiting.

Betty Firth was pleased with the turn-out. It had taken only a word or two, a little encouragement, the odd reminder. It had been a busy afternoon but the fair-sized crowd in the village hall was ample reward.

She glanced at her watch; it was so important to start on time. The Unit had a showing in Patfield when they'd finished in Shevington. She caught the eye of the young soldier who operated the projector which had been set up in the aisle between the lines of chairs and he nodded. Betty nodded back. It was all rather exciting.

The villagers watched as she secured the black-out blinds over the windows. In the gloom the projector clattered irritably before settling to an even hum. For a moment the grey canvas screen filled with an empty square of light; and then, as the fanfare sounded, it began to darken and flicker into life.

The crowd were pressed each side of the narrow, cobbled street as the procession wound its way down the hill from the castle. The big wooden cart was escorted by small children in white tunics linked to each other with ropes of flowers. There were flowers everywhere: crowning the horns of the oxen that pulled the cart along, decorating its poles and swaying canopy, and entwined in the hair of the beautiful young women who stood beneath it scattering rose-petals as they passed. Behind the cart rode a company of knights in shining armour, with plumes tossing on their helmets and long pennants fluttering from their lances; their horses were draped with colourful silks and chivalric cloths; and their shields were fierce with eagles, bears, and prancing leopards. As they passed,

71

the crowd raised a sea of small swastika flags and threw their hats in the air.

A bright evening sun shone low in the sky lengthening the shadows of the men on the hill. There were four of them: General von Schreier and three of his close staff. They were guarded by two armed soldiers who watched from the tangle of concrete and metal which had once been an anti-aircraft emplacement on the crest above.

A church clock began to strike the hour. The four men raised their binoculars and trained them on the village which lay in the hollow below. Middelbury: a small, flint-faced church with a squat, square tower, a dozen or so cottages, and the narrow road which, following the foot of the Downs, ran through it. The soldiers waiting in lorries parked each end of the village jumped down and began running from house to house, hammering at the doors with their rifle butts, and ordering those inside into the street. The villagers were herded towards the church and assembled in front of the lych-gate. Then the soldiers formed up in line opposite and waited. They waited until the clock sounded the quarter hour. Then a military staff car drove up accompanied by an open-topped lorry. SS Hauptsturmführer Honegger got out of the car followed by an army officer and walked across to the line of soldiers.

The two men stood side by side slowly scanning the faces in the crowd.

'What's this all in aid of?' demanded a woman near the front. 'You've got no cause to treat us like this.'

'I have to inform you,' the SS man spoke quietly, almost casually, 'that unless the perpetrators of the recent terrorist outrage either surrender in person or are identified to me immediately, four male prisoners will be taken at random and held until such time as the matter is resolved.'

In the stunned silence that followed an elderly man in carpet-slippers stepped into the road. 'But you can't,' he said. 'You can't punish people for something they haven't done.'

A child began to cry and its mother quickly gathered its face into her skirt.

'How are we s'posed to know who they are?' someone asked.

'Now look here, officer,' said the man in the slippers.

'Don't, Charlie!' A woman came out of the crowd and tugged at his sleeve. 'Leave it alone, please.'

But he would not be silenced. 'Good God, man, this is downright . . . it's downright savagery!'

Honegger did not reply. He looked across at the silent, frightened faces by the lych-gate, and waited. Finally, he looked at his watch. 'I see no purpose in prolonging this matter,' he said. He nodded to the officer standing beside him who then signalled to the men waiting by the truck. They let down the tailboard and it fell with a crash. Honegger indicated the old man in front of him and at once two soldiers took hold of him and, pushing his wife to one side, bundled him away. Other soldiers had gone into the crowd and, selecting three men at random, they dragged them off towards the truck. The villagers pressed forward, calling out to the prisoners. The officer barked a command and there was an ominous rattle, like dominoes falling, as the line of troops released the safety-catches on their rifles. The villagers fell back. All except for a red-faced young man with sandy hair. Ted Naylor had been drinking in the snug of The Middelbury Beacon when the soldiers came and still had his glass in his hand.

Honegger and his companion watched as the young man looked round, and then, placing his glass carefully on the ground, stepped forward.

'Take me,' he said, 'not old Charlie Dawson. He ain't been well. You take me instead.'

'Hauptsturmführer?' said the officer.

SS Hauptsturmführer Honegger thought for a moment, and then shook his head. 'No,' he said, 'not you.'

Ted Naylor raised his fist, but was felled instantly by a blow from a rifle-butt.

The Hauptsturmführer surveyed the frightened, angry faces watching by the lych-gate. 'This is not an occasion for futile heroics,' he said. 'Information is all I require. Names. You will otherwise leave me with only one alternative.' The men by the truck began to bundle their prisoners aboard. Honegger and the officer turned and walked over to their car, which then drove away. The line of soldiers divided and went slowly back the way they had come. By the time the clock struck the half-hour the operation was complete.

The old woman lifted the young man's head and wiped the blood from his face. 'You tried, Ted,' she said. 'You couldn't have done more.'

On the hill above the village the wind had risen. As he made his way down the track to his car, General von Schreier turned up the collar of his greatcoat.

'So changeable, this English weather,' he observed.

'That we cannot control, Herr General.'

'No, Werner. But give the Hauptsturmführer long enough and I imagine he will certainly try.'

Frank looked across to the table beside the projector where the cans of film had been piled. It was empty. It wouldn't be long now.

It had been just what he'd expected. Newsreels mostly. And a short film about the German Red Cross and how nice they were to everyone. But mostly newsreels: Hitler arriving at some theatre, and watching a load of Vikings singing, and then shaking hands with them; polite Dutch children presenting armfuls of tulips to grinning German sailors; Hitler being shown a new road—straight as an arrow to the

74

heart! Wasn't that what Sims had said? He was right—this one was going from Berlin to Paris; a factory somewhere up North—Leeds or somewhere—where they were being entertained in the canteen by that famous comedian. He'd sung a song and told them how important it was to keep their sense of humour—a lot of people in the village hall had laughed at that; and those knights in armour, of course; and Hitler giving medals to paratroopers and showing them a huge map of what looked like Russia.

Frank looked at the faces caught in the flickering light. He wondered what Firth had said to them. She couldn't have promised them all to have letters from their husbands. He glanced at Edie, who was sitting the other side of Nan; she had a faraway look on her face. She'd put her best dress on and a hat he never knew she had, the sort Robin Hood used to wear. That was what hope did to people. And what about the ones who'd stayed away from Betty and her stupid films? They'd been given hope too. That hand-grenade at Middelbury had given them hope. And his hope? His hope was that perhaps . . . perhaps, something was beginning—at last.

The Stuka dive-bombers wheeled again above the burning city and dropped, shrieking, from the leaden sky. In the rubble below, hunched figures sprinted for the cover of a doorway as the distance erupted in smoke and fire. The front of one tall, elegant building seemed simply to peel away and topple slowly into the street below.

Above the chatter of machine-guns the voice of the commentator continued its exultant, breathless harangue:

'Inexorably, on every front, the armies of the Reich strike, each blow more deadly than the last, deeper and deeper into the Bolshevik heartland!'

A tank rose steeply on a pile of stones and plunged down again pursued by the infantry hurrying in its wake.

Suddenly the screen was filled with waving corn. And moving through it, down a long road that descended and then rose again, was an endless line of troops and vehicles.

'Day after day, overwhelming all before them!' The commentator's voice trembled with emotion. 'Ever onward. Until it shall be truly said: the Reich will stretch from farthest steppe to setting sun . . . and last a thousand years!'

The music swelled to a resounding chord, cymbals crashed, the picture shuddered, flickered, and became a blank, white glare.

Chapter 6

'Is there something you would like to say to the children, Mr Forbes-Handley?'

The Inspector, who had been provided with a chair on the platform at the end of the hall, looked up at the headmaster and shook his head. He was a grey, bespectacled figure with a large black briefcase clutched on his lap.

Mr Underwood nodded. 'Very well.' And paused for a moment, considering the faces gazing up at him. 'Before I send you off to your lessons,' he said, 'there is something I want to say to you. And I want you all to listen very carefully. Some of you may have already heard what happened over in Middelbury last night.' He saw one or two of them nodding. 'And if you have, I expect you have been talking to each other about it. These matters can become very confused, so I want you to know the plain facts. Last evening, the SS, aided and abetted by General von Schreier's soldiers . . . '

Mr Forbes-Handley began to shift uneasily on his chair. Miss Meacher looked across at Mr Sims, but he seemed unaware of the danger of the situation. He also looked as though he'd slept badly; he certainly seemed to have dressed in a hurry: the normally so-precise knot in his college tie was all askew, and his shirt collar was turned up on one side. Today of all days! But it was Mr Underwood who was the immediate problem. These Ministry people were bound to be government men, and Mr Underwood was being rather foolhardy. Foolhardy, but very brave.

77

'. . . surrounded Middelbury and seized four innocent men as hostages against the discovery of those who attacked their soldiers the other night. I say, "seized", children, because they were not arrested—they couldn't be arrested because they have committed no crime—they have been taken quite at random, imprisoned, and threatened with death. This was done to terrorize us, to make us frightened.'

The Inspector cleared his throat noisily and took out his watch, but Mr Underwood would not be intimidated.

'And it is a frightening thing. But above all it is a wicked thing. It is wicked and wrong and can never be right whatever and by whoever you may be told to the contrary. That is the most important and the simplest thing to remember. This was a wicked and evil deed. As long as you remember that such wickedness cannot prevail. That is all I want to say to you.' Mr Underwood took out his own watch. 'Lessons today,' he said, 'will be just as normal. Our visitor must take us as he finds us. Thank you, children. Good morning.'

'Good morning, Mr Underwood,' they chorused.

Whenever the wireless speaker was brought down the corridor from the headmaster's room the cable came adrift; but Mr Sims seemed to be having even more trouble than usual re-plugging it. And, what was more, he didn't look well.

'Went the colour of that chalk,' said Wally Carr, 'soon as he saw the Inspector.'

'It was our dad seen him first,' said Nat Gingell. 'Come in home and told us he'd seen that Inspector first thing s'morning, driving his car down past the other side of Thrales'. That was early on.'

George Poole grinned. 'Come early to catch the worm, I reckon.'

'What d'you reckon he's got in that big black case of his?' said Wally.

'Hard questions,' said Nat; 'bound to be.'

But if Mr Forbes-Handley's bag was full of hard questions, they didn't seem to be for the pupils of Shevington School. After Assembly, he passed briefly through the classrooms with hardly a word, and then retired to the headmaster's room where he had been ever since.

'Him and Mr Underwood's deciding what to do with the Toff,' Nat Gingell concluded.

And George Poole agreed. 'What d'you reckon then, Nat? Hanging or the bullet?'

'Quiet! Quiet, everyone!' Peter Sims emerged from behind the speaker. 'Be quiet, please. It's about to start. Please, be quiet!'

The final chord of Elgar's Second Symphony died to a whisper and the weekly Broadcast to British Schools began:

'Good morning, boys and girls of Britain.' The voice was unmistakably English: cultivated, slightly halting. 'This morning I want to talk to you very seriously about Duty. I want to talk to you about the duty we must assume, each and every one of us, to build anew. To forge a future that is clean and noble. To construct a New Order purged of all degenerate or destructive elements and raised on the sure foundations of our ceaseless Vigilance and Will. I am speaking, boys and girls of Britain, of our duty to rebuild the world.'

'Sir?'

Sims had returned to his desk and was sitting there with his head in his hands.

'Sir?'

'What is it?'

'Sir, it's Marge, sir,' said the girl next to Marge Prout. 'She's gone ever so hot.'

'Has she? Well, tell her to . . . tell her to sit still,' he said absently, 'that's the best thing to do.'

'There are, of course,' said the voice from the speaker, 'those who will urge you at every opportunity: look back! Who will assure you that what is good, what is best, can only be what-used-to-be. Boys and girls of Britain, they lie! Don't be deceived. Don't be drawn into their nets. Pay them not one moment's heed. Look forward! Always look forward. You live, boys and girls of Britain, at the most exciting time in the history of the world.'

Frank tipped back his chair and rested his head against the wall.

It was always the same. If it wasn't Duty it was Discipline, or Sacrifice, or something similar. And, without fail, the voice from the speaker always told them how lucky they were, the boys and girls of Britain; and what a wonderful life was waiting for them—if they behaved themselves. And how did they behave? How did the Germans behave? Just like Mr Underwood said—they took hostages. And that was against the law. Colin had run upstairs and looked it up in his encyclopaedia straight after breakfast when Jack Cowdrey had dropped into Nan's cottage with the news. It was against the Geneva Convention. It said so in black and white. Or so Colin said. He'd read it out to them.

Frank glanced out of the window. A sleek, grey staff-car was approaching the checkpoint on the other side of the Green. It wasn't one he recognized. They all knew the big Mercedes-Benz cars from the Hall. Colin could recite them, numbers and insignia, like a party-piece. Nan sometimes used to ask him to. But this one was new. Two men in dark caps and uniforms got out and went into the hut. Frank nudged Les but his eyes were closed and his chin was resting on his chest. Nothing much ever seemed to bother Les. He could always just shut himself off. Across the Green the driver had got out and was standing by the bonnet. Frank formed his fingers into a pistol, took careful aim, and: Bang! he mouthed silently.

Keeper Thrale unhooked the noose of wire from the twigs and dropped it into his game-bag. Before the war he would have known, give or take a man or two, who the poacher might have been; he might even have recognized the way the snare was tied—that could sometimes be as good as a fingerprint. This wasn't one he knew. It could have been anyone, of course. There were plenty these days who'd be pleased to have some extra meat on the table: to have any meat at all. But he was fly, this one—whoever he was, there wasn't a footprint to be seen.

Alec picked up his bag and moved on through the undergrowth. Some fifty yards or so from where he had discovered the snare he emerged into a small clearing. As he did so, he stopped and listened. Then he slipped quietly back into cover. He waited, then, as the figure emerged from the undergrowth on the other side of the clearing, he snapped his shotgun into place and stepped from the trees.

'What are you doing here?' he demanded.

SS Hauptsturmführer Honegger turned. He showed no sign of surprise or alarm. 'Ah,' he said, 'Herr Thrale. Good day. Please point your weapon elsewhere.'

Thrale lowered his gun. 'I could have shot you for a poacher,' he said.

'I think I would have shot you first,' the Hauptsturmführer replied calmly. And from the trees behind the keeper came two armed soldiers, one preceded by an Alsatian dog.

'What's that damned dog doing here?' Thrale said angrily. 'Good God, man, I've got birds nesting in these covers! The General's going to hear about this.'

'Contain yourself, Herr Thrale. I am simply making my rounds. You are a policeman, too—of a kind; you must realize how important it is to be acquainted with one's beat.'

'You should have warned me.'

'I never give warnings, Herr Thrale,' Honegger replied. 'That would rather defeat the object of the exercise, don't you think?'

'If you're coming into these woods there's matters require discussion.'

'I do not think so. During the celebrations for the Führer's birthday I am extending the patrols around Shevington Hall. It is quite simple. These woods are no exception. Good day, Herr Thrale.' Honegger signalled to the soldiers and they began to move away. 'Oh,' he turned back as though he had forgotten something. 'Herr Thrale,' he said, 'your gun.'

'What about my gun?'

'I have spoken to General von Schreier. For the moment you may continue to keep it. Good day again. *Heil Hitler.*'

Alec Thrale watched them go. 'I hope it's you they're after, my lad,' he said softly. 'By God, I do hope it's you they're after.'

'The Britain of King Alfred, of Drake and Wellington,' said the voice from the speaker. 'The Britain of Milton, Tennyson, and Dickens. But a Britain, too, that is proud to takes its place as the Western Bastion of the New European Order. Resolve this moment, boys and girls, to go forward with that historic process, to march side by side . . . '

'Sir? Sir?'

Marge Prout had her hand up but Sims didn't seem to have noticed.

'Please, sir,' she said desperately. 'I do, I feel ever so hot.'

'For goodness' sake, child!' Sims snapped. 'Do what you're told! Just keep still and listen. Is that quite beyond you? Don't you know who this man is?' He pointed to the wireless speaker. 'He is a very famous man. An acclaimed author. Is it too much to ask you to give him your attention for fifteen minutes?' He glared round at their bewildered faces. No one had ever seen the Toff lose his temper before. 'All you're asked to do is . . . ' He shook his head and looked away. 'All you're asked to do is look as though you're listening.'

George Poole drew a finger across his throat and there was some giggling.

'Collaboration?' asked the voice from the speaker. 'Is fighting for your country's future "collaboration"? No, never say so! The men and women who toil night and day towards that goal are not collaborators. The collaborators are the moral and physical hooligans who strive unceasingly to endanger that future with their adventures and violence. I speak of the cowards who burn and kill in a name to which they have no right. That name is Patriotism. And those cowards are the men and women who collaborate with ruin, with disorder, and with death—the men and women who call themselves the Resistance! What is it they resist? Rebirth? Renewal? Hope? Oh, boys and girls of Britain, let me warn you from the bottom of my heart . . . '

But the famous person's heartfelt warning went unheard among the groans and frantic scraping of chairs as Marge Prout was suddenly sick all over her desk.

Miss Meacher was called and came and took Marge away; and everyone else was sent outside. Except Frank and Les, who were on speaker-duty.

'Did you hear him?' said Frank eagerly, as they carried the speaker back along the corridor. 'Did you hear what he said?'

'Who?'

'The Voice?'

'I wasn't listening.'

'He was going on about the Resistance. I mean, when did they ever mention the Resistance before? It's Middelbury that's done it, Les.'

'And look what happened to them.'

'But it's not just Middelbury. People must be fighting back in more places than Middelbury for them to bother to go on about it so much as that!'

'They always go on about things. They go on about everything.'

'Les, the Schools Broadcast goes all over the country, the same one. There must be people all over the country making trouble for them; fighting back. That's what it means.'

They knocked at the headmaster's door and were told to wait.

'Think the Inspector's still in there?' said Frank.

Les frowned. 'Why don't we just leave the speaker outside, eh?'

'We can't do that, not now we've knocked.'

'Come in.'

'Bringing back the speaker, sir,' said Frank.

Mr Underwood nodded. 'Thank you, Tate. You know where it goes.'

'Do your staff find the broadcasts a useful tool, Mr Underwood?' Mr Forbes-Handley was sitting opposite the headmaster. Seen from the back row in Assembly that morning he had seemed a much older man: Frank was surprised to see that he wasn't very much older than Sims. 'Their object is, of course, to inspire. Do you find the broadcasts inspiring, young man?'

'Me, sir?' said Frank.

'You, sir.'

Frank saw the anxiety on Mr Underwood's face. But the headmaster needn't have worried. 'Oh, yes, sir,' he said enthusiastically. 'I thought the one this morning was pie-hot!'

'It was what?'

'It cheered me up, sir—no end!'

'Well, I suppose that is a form of inspiration. And your companion,' the Inspector turned to Les, 'what did he think of it?'

'What Frank said,' said Les.

'Pie-hot?' said the Inspector.

'Yeah. I thought that too.'

84

'Not a local boy, Mr Underwood?' said the Inspector turning back to the headmaster.

'Leslie Gill? No, Inspector. He's from London.'

'I thought as much. Although it wouldn't take Professor Higgins to place that cockney twang. And what brought you to Shevington, Gill?'

'I walked, sir.'

'From London?'

'No, sir.'

'Then where did you walk from?'

'I can't remember.'

'Were you an evacuee? Was that it?'

Les shrugged.

Forbes-Handley turned away. 'I've seen it before, Mr Underwood,' he observed. 'Their minds are blessed with an astonishing capacity to shut out the horrors they may have encountered. It's the memory's way of binding up the wounds.'

'Quite,' said Mr Underwood. 'Run along both of you. That's if you've no more questions, Inspector?'

'No,' said the Inspector. 'No more questions.'

'Smug toad,' said Frank once they were back in the corridor. 'Why didn't you tell him?'

'Tell him what?'

'What happened to you. About the sweet shop.'

'What d'you mean?'

'You know, Crocker's, where you lived when you were evacuated: about it being hit by that German shell and only you and Mill escaping. That would have told him, all right!'

'Nah,' said Les. 'Nah. Answer one stupid question and his sort just goes on asking you loads more.'

Out in the playground a crowd had gathered by the railings facing The Green.

As Frank and Les came out into the yard Colin called to them and pointed: 'They've taken over the checkpoint. See them?"

The dark-uniformed men Frank had seen arriving

earlier were now standing at the barrier, which had been lowered and where a queue was already forming.

'Hans, "Knees", and "Bumpsadaisy" have gone,' said Wally Carr. 'They came and took 'em off in a lorry.'

'Them two's stopping everybody,' said Lib Ferris. 'Look at 'em—searching in their bags and everything. Don't they look grim?'

''Course they do,' said Colin, 'they're SS, aren't they! With the death's head on their caps.'

'The what?'

'The skull and crossbones.'

'What, like pirates?'

'And they'll have the double lightning flash on their collars. They started out as Hitler's personal bodyguards, you know. Always in black. Responsible for the pursuit of the Nazis' political enemies . . . that sort of thing.'

'Know what you sound like, Colin Worth?' said Wally Carr. 'A flippin' book.'

'Or a parrot,' said George Poole.

'That doesn't mean it isn't true,' said Colin. 'They're like Hauptsturmführer Honegger up at the Hall. They'll be under his orders, I expect.'

'It must be 'cos of the goings-on,' said Lib Ferris. 'All them Nasty toffs and such coming to the party.'

'No,' said Frank. 'That ain't it.' And everyone turned to look at him. 'It's 'cos of what happened over in Middelbury. That's what's put the wind up them.'

'Do what?' George Poole laughed. 'You'm weak in the head, Frank Tate. Look at 'em! Don't look like they got the wind up to me.'

''Course they don't,' said Colin. 'Not the SS. They're the Nazis' pie-hot men.'

Miss Meacher's heart sank when she opened the envelope Betty Firth had sent down to the school mid-morning:

A Song for The Day
words by
Adrian Bowen-Doughty
music by
Gilda Probert LRAM

She sighed as she read the instruction printed over the opening bars: 'tempo di marcia.' Didn't the heirs of Schubert and Brahms, she wondered, do anything any more that wasn't in march time? Her music was Audrey Meacher's great solace. She would often spend whole evenings seated at the piano in the front room of the cottage she and her mother shared out on the Patfield Road, drifting dreamily through her repertoire. And even at the battered keyboard in the hall at Shevington School her gentle, wistful playing had convinced one or two of the older girls that she must have lost her young man in the war. She hadn't; but there were times when Audrey felt as though she had.

Warden Firth had attached a note to the score suggesting that since time was short the sooner the choir began to rehearse the better. So Miss Meacher had seized the first opportunity. Besides, it had occurred to her that the sounds of rehearsal might impress the awful Mr Forbes-Handley and keep him from submitting a too critical report. He really was a pompous ass. He'd even had the gall to ask the headmaster to vacate his office; he was in there now—with poor Peter Sims.

Miss Meacher took them slowly through The Song, line by line, teaching them the tune and words. The afternoon was warm for the time of year, and their faces became redder and redder as they tramped through verse and chorus, mile after mile:

'Beneath the banner that flies before us,
Under skies of blazing light,
We will raise our voice in chorus,
As we hurry to the fight,' they sang.

'Key change!' Miss Meacher called from the piano.

'Remember the key change, everyone!'
                    'Where the foe may seek to bar us
                    And the enemy holds sway,
                    We will hurl them down before us,
                    Make a world that's ours for aye!
                    We will build! Build anew!
                    Build a world that's clean and strong.
                    Where the mountains soar and the rivers run,
                    When the battle's fought and the day is won,
                    From the farthest steppe to the setting sun,
                    Let them hear!
                    Let them hear our marching song.'

Mile after mile they tramped, stamping out the rhythm as they went. And Audrey Meacher was relieved when the urgent hand waving to her by the window allowed her to lift her hands from the keys.

'Yes, Libby?'

'Mr Sims, miss.'

'What about him?'

'Out in the yard, miss.'

Everyone turned to the window; and even Miss Meacher found she was looking anxiously to where Mr Sims and the Inspector stood talking not far from the school gates.

'Got the poke has he, miss?' George Poole enquired casually.

'Don't be impertinent,' she replied. But it rather looked as if he had. And she couldn't help feeling a little sorry for him. He wasn't at all cut out for a small country school like Shevington, with his Latin tags and college ways. But he had tried.

'You were perfectly aware from the beginning what would be expected of you,' said the Inspector, opening the door of his car. 'If you didn't think you were up to it you should have spoken then.'

Sims nodded wearily. 'I know. It's come as something of a shock, that's all.'

'The decision has been made and there's an end to it.'

'Of course, Tommy. It's just that I've been so . . . so out of everything here, that's all. I'm not sure I can . . . '

'For goodness' sake, Peter, pull yourself together!' Mr Forbes-Handley got into his car and slammed the door. 'You'll be hearing from me,' he said, 'very soon.' And with that he drove away out of the yard.

'If you please, children!' Miss Meacher clapped her hands for attention and immediately wished she hadn't.

Peter Sims looked up and saw the faces turning from the window and knew they had been watching. He had never felt so utterly alone. And there's an end to it. Wasn't that what 'Tommy' Forbes-Handley had said? Yes, it was an end right enough. An end to his rustic idyll. To '*Dulce somnum sub arbore et mugitus boum*'—to 'Sleeping sweetly under the trees to the lowing of kine'. What a rude awakening!

The singing had begun again and he stood in the empty playground listening as the voices came drifting through the open window.

> 'It is the Führer alone who guides us
> And who shows the way ahead.
> Adolf Hitler is here beside us,
> Forward, comrades, without dread!'

'Key change, everyone! Remember the key change!'

Chapter 7

Mill Gill frowned as she gave the mixture a cautious stir. The apple bark had boiled and simmered for two hours and more, and it had certainly turned the water green; but Mill still wasn't convinced. Earlier, Vera had made the other mixture—What was it she called it? The mordant: to make sure the colour stayed fast and didn't fade. And then she had taken the beautiful frock, and, to Mill's horror, dropped it into it. And any minute now, when this lot was cool, she was going to drop it into this as well. And boil it up!

'Lichens for brown or copper colours, privet leaves for yellow, blackberries for blue, and apple bark for green. You see, Mildred, the fields and hedgerows are teeming with leaves and berries and barks which can provide us with every imaginable colour. The opportunities for transformation are endless.'

Trust Vera to know something like that. But then, Vera Thrale knew so many things. Vera was an educated person. Though, to be fair, she was good at explaining things as well: good at telling you things, making sense of them so you remembered them. Like that mordant business. And the other thing, perhaps? The thing that was bothering Mill no end, again? It had been worrying her now for days. Yes—Vera would certainly be the one to explain it, to make sense of it. But Mill knew it was something she couldn't ask her—not that. Why, when things seemed to be settling down, when she'd really begun to think her and Les might be safe, why had them Crockers started coming to mind again? Why was that?

90

'Cos they had. She'd even mentioned it to Les; but he'd dismissed it, like it didn't make no odds, or like he'd forgotten all about them. But Mill hadn't. Bert and Dot Crocker: Crocker's Korner Kiosk! Living in that sweet shop wasn't something anyone could forget in a hurry.

Bert and Dot had been the last ones to come. By early evening there were only Mill and Les left still unclaimed in the church hall near the railway station. There had been fifty evacuees all told who'd left London early that morning for the safety of the country. That was a laugh. Dot Crocker was a bloody sight more dangerous than any Dornier bomber. But that was later.

The first night, when they'd stopped in front of the shop window and Bert had begun to fumble for his keys, Mill and Les couldn't believe their luck.

'Is this where you really live?' Les asked.

'That's right,' said Bert.

'Bloody hell!'

'Language! thank you, young man,' said Dot.

The window was full of them: jars, packets, tins, and boxes, more sweets than they had ever seen.

But as time passed, they began to notice the dust on the jars and the empty shelves inside the shop. And the fact that the bell above the door rang less and less as the months passed. And that most of the nineteen shillings which was their billeting allowance went over the counter of the Bottle and Jug down at The Berkshire Fusilier. And that Dot spent more and more time sitting in the front room cussing Bert and eating her way through what was left of the stock.

Then the bashing started. Just Mill; Dot Crocker never touched Les. It might be because something hadn't been dusted, or the teapot hadn't been warmed, anything at all really. She was sorry afterwards: 'I am, dear, I am so sorry,' she'd say. 'I'm a bad woman. Here—take them all.' And shove a box of chocolates at her. And then she'd cry. But it didn't stop her doing it the next time. She even bashed her the day the letter

91

came from London. She bashed her then because Mill hadn't cried when she heard that there'd been no survivors after the bomb hit the house down by the docks where she and Les had lived.

'You got to tell somebody,' Les had urged her. 'It ain't right, Mill.'

'And what if they believe me? They'll want to move us, won't they!'

''Course they will.'

'Yes. And who's going to take the two of us, eh? They'll split us up, Les. And I ain't having that.'

'We'll make a run for it, then.'

'No, it'll be all right. I'll cope.'

But they had run for it. In the end they'd had to. Sleeping rough. Staying away from the main roads as much as they could. Going into towns occasionally to get grub from the Red Cross Feeding Stations. Keeping their heads down. Till the day they knocked on Vera's door.

'Miles away, Mildred?'

Mill jumped. 'Sorry, Mrs Thrale.'

'That looks perfect,' said Vera, peering into the bucket. She looked up at Mill. 'Were you thinking about those poor men over at Middelbury?'

'Middelbury, Mrs Thrale?'

'I haven't been able to get them out of my mind.'

'Still, the Jerries can't do nothing to them, can they? I mean, they ain't done nothing.'

'Their innocence won't stop the General and his SS friends, Mildred. The Nazis' philosophy has very little to do with justice, of any sort.'

'P'raps whoever it was shouldn't have blown them soldiers up,' said Mill.

'Oh, no,' said Vera, 'I think we have to be quite muscular about that.' She had brought the frock with her and a large piece of muslin cloth, which she now proceeded to shake out. 'People have the right, even the duty, to resist,' she said. 'We must never let tyranny overwhelm us. No, Mildred, we have to resist them.' Vera smiled. 'In whatever way we can.' She took the muslin and placed it across the top of the dye in the bucket.

'And what's that for?' Mill asked.

'That will separate the garment from the bark. Reach me my frock, there's a dear.'

Mill held the frock out to her. 'It's a lovely frock,' she said.

'Yes—it has always been a favourite of mine.'

'Mrs Thrale?'

'Yes?'

'Have you done this before?'

Vera Thrale smiled. 'Oh, yes,' she said, 'lots of times. Look here, would you like us to dye something of yours? One of your woollies?' Mill shook her head doubtfully. 'Wouldn't you like something new for the celebrations? I'm sure I've another dress somewhere we could alter for you. Wouldn't you like a change?'

'No,' said Mill, 'I'd better not. You really sure it's going to go green, Mrs Thrale?' she added, watching anxiously as Vera lowered the frock into the dye.

'We'll just have to bring it back to the boil and see,' said Vera. 'Of course, it's not the most exact science, but it can be terribly effective. Really quite vivid. We must be vivid on The Day, don't you think?' She saw Mill's anxious expression. 'Don't worry so, Mildred.'

'I do worry,' Mill replied. 'I can't help it.'

'Yes. I'd noticed.'

'But it don't mean I'm miserable or nothing,' she added hastily.

Vera smiled again. 'I'm so glad,' she said.

'From the farthest steppe to the setting sun,
We will build! Build anew!'

'The Song for The Day' shuffled to a halt.

'Well done, everyone,' said Miss Meacher. 'You are doing awfully well.'

93

'Quite well, Miss Meacher; but they must listen to the music.'

'Miss Firth?'

Warden Firth was sitting beside the piano in the school hall. She had arrived just after dinnertime and insisted on hearing what progress the choir had made. She was feeling anxious: the unpleasantness over at Middelbury seemed to have cast a pall over the village; and an especial effort would have to be made to restore morale if The Day was to be the success she was determined it would. It was true, her preparations for the celebrations looked fine on paper, and the General's office had given them the go-ahead; Mr Dearman had assured her he was organizing the Scouts' parade, and she had promises that the 'groaning board' of home-made foods would appear on the day; and so, for the moment, the choir was the only thing she could actually do anything about.

'They must let the music speak to them, Miss Meacher.'

'Speak to them?'

'I am not a musician, Miss Meacher, but it occurs to me that those last lines are meant to be a paean of triumph, an affirmation of a golden future. They should soar!'

'Soar?'

'I can't hear it yet.'

Audrey Meacher stiffened. This was going too far. There had been a time, when Betty Firth had first returned to Shevington, when Audrey had felt quite sorry for her; Audrey had an invalid parent of her own and had known what it must have cost her to give up her job in London and come home to nurse that father of hers. That was all very sad. But there was a limit! Sitting there looking so superior, as though that wretched armband had suddenly transformed her from the nosy busybody she had always been into an authority on everything under the

sun. Betty Firth had about as much music in her as
. . . as that floorboard!

'I wonder, Miss Firth, if perhaps we should shout the
final chorus?'

The Warden and the choir stared at her. 'Shout it,
Miss Meacher?'

'At the top of our voices. I'm sure that would help us
catch the spirit of the thing more precisely,' said Miss
Meacher. 'Come along, everyone. Without the music
this time. The final chorus. As loud as you possibly can.'

'But, miss?' asked a small boy at the front.

'Yes, Stanley?'

'If we shout, miss, everybody'll hear us.'

'That's right. I shall count to three. One-two-three!

'We will build! Build anew!

Build a world that's clean and strong,' they roared.

'Where the mountains soar and the rivers run,

When the battle's fought and the day is won,

From the farthest steppe to the setting sun

We will build—build anew!'

'Bravo! Bravo!' Betty Firth applauded enthusiastically.
'My word, but that's the spirit of the thing—there's no
question about it! Well done, all of you.' She looked up
at the clock on the wall. 'Oh, dear—just when it was
starting to go so well,' she said. 'I'm afraid I'm going to
have to leave you all. But before I do, I would like to say
a few words to spur you on to even greater efforts. This
splendid song has, as you know, been specially written
for The Day. It will be sung by choirs large and small
throughout the country, in cities, towns, and tiny
hamlets. Just think of it—all those voices united as
one. I know that as you look around you you may be
tempted to think: but we are few. Not so. Always
remember that you will be part of a greater choir and a
unique moment. A moment I am sure you will all
remember for the rest of your lives. Thank you, Miss
Meacher. Please continue the good work. I'll just slip
away. Pay me no heed.'

No heed at all, Miss Firth! As the Warden left the hall, Audrey Meacher took a small lace handkerchief from her pocket and dabbed at her cheek.

'Miss?'

'What is it, Stanley?'

'We ain't going to sing it like that, are we, miss?'

'No, Stanley,' she said firmly, 'we are not. If we have to sing it at all, then we are going to sing it properly.'

Betty Firth hurried across The Green. She felt so much better. It had been a wise decision to go down to the school. It had cheered her up. Renewed her enthusiasm. How splendid The Song had sounded—eventually. It was so rewarding, so satisfying to be able to help. Though there had been an odd moment by the piano when Miss Meacher had seemed . . . What? Well, not quite herself. Yes, there was no question about it, she had seemed almost . . . yes, terse. Highly-strung, of course—like so many so-called artistic folk. Which was why they so often missed the point. Couldn't see the wood for the trees.

And quickening her pace, Betty crossed the road and pushed open the door of Dearman's Stores.

'Here I am, Mr Dearman,' she beamed. 'I just thought I'd pop in and go over the details of the Scouts' contribution with you.'

It certainly didn't look as though Mr Forbes-Handley had given Peter Sims the poke. And though, even some days later, he still looked what Wally Carr called 'shook', he was going about his lessons as normal. He had almost finished taking the older ones for sums that afternoon, when Deb Gingell came in from the yard and announced: 'Yur! Know what they're doing? They're digging up The Green!'

'Who?' demanded half a dozen voices all at once. 'Who are?'

'The Jerries.'

They were in the wrong room to be able to look out and see for themselves, and so several hands went up right away and asked to be excused. But Sims wouldn't let them go and they were forced to wait impatiently while he filled the last ten minutes or so with more imaginary shopping-lists—mostly of items they hadn't seen in Dearman's window for months—pints, ounces, and change from a pound.

When the bell finally sounded everyone ran out to the gate. A lorry loaded with long wooden poles was parked in the middle of The Green. Two poles had already been put up, and a third was being manoeuvred into position by four civilians, who were watched over by a couple of German soldiers. On one of the poles was a loudspeaker from which hung a coiled cable.

'We're going to have to listen to Hitler whether we want to or not,' said Frank, as he and Les started across The Green.

'Shouldn't think he'd need no loudspeaker the way he carries on.'

'No, not even from Berlin.'

The four men positioning the final pole were raggedly dressed; their faces were thin and hungry-looking, and their hair was closely cropped like convicts. They were talking amongst themselves as Frank and Les went by. It wasn't German, Frank decided; but whatever it was he couldn't understand it, and when one of them spoke to him he could only hesitate and shrug. The man spoke again; and it was then one of the others, a small man in a dirty singlet and canvas trousers, looked up from his shovel.

'Good God Almighty!' he said, staring at Frank. 'It never is! It is—it's you, en't it!'

'Me?'

'I know you; I know you, don't I?'

Frank stared back at him. That gaunt, bearded face wasn't a face he knew. But there was something about the voice.

97

'It's me, lad! Don't you remember me? Yorkie!'

Yorkie? Yorkie? The soldier he'd last seen all those months ago in Seabourne—the afternoon when he'd gone off to meet his dad from the bus? The one who had waved to him from the Prom? The corporal from Yorkshire him and his dad used to chat to! 'Yorkie!'

'Aye! Don't come too close. They don't like us hobnobbin' wi' locals.'

'Yorkie, what are you doing here?'

'I'd not a lot of say in the matter.'

'*Engländer!*' The soldier came across from the lorry and pointed to a large bucket. '*Wasser,*' he said, '*schnell!*'

Yorkie stuck his shovel into the ground. 'And how the hell am I supposed to know where the water is?'

'Me,' said Frank quickly. He pointed to himself, then to his eyes, then to Yorkie. 'I can show him.'

The soldier called to his companion who was talking to the lorry driver and who nodded in reply. 'So,' he said. 'You go with the boy. *Schnell, verstanden?*'

'*Verstanden,*' said Yorkie, grabbing the bucket. 'Come on, lad, lively. That one's allus on my back. It's 'cos I'm playing at home, I reckon. All the rest are Dutchmen. Politicals.'

They crossed The Green and everyone in the playground stood back and watched as they hurried to the tap. Yorkie placed the bucket under the spout and turned it on.

'Slow like,' he winked. 'It'll give us a minute to jaw. By! but I couldn't believe my eyes, seeing you like that. I did, I thought—it can't be!'

'Are you a prisoner of war?'

The soldier scooped a handful of water and let it trickle over his face. 'I were,' he said, 'for a bit. But I went on the run. Once you do that they don't bother much wi' the rules any more. Still, we've survived, eh, lad? That's the important thing. But what are you doing here? I thought you and your dad lived in Seabourne?'

'I'm living with my gran,' said Frank. 'Dad's dead.'

'Dammit all, but that's bad luck. I'm sorry to hear that.'

'He was killed the night they came.'

'How d'you mean, the night they came?'

'He was fire-watching at the factory where he worked: Bell's Precision. He never came back.'

'That's as maybe, lad,' said Yorkie, 'but he weren't killed. Not the night they came.'

'Yes, he was fire-watching at the factory.'

'Happen he were but . . . Look here, that's what took me back so, you see . . . when I saw you. I mean, that were rare enough . . . but I'd seen him and all, not more'n a month since. Your dad's not dead. I've seen him.'

'You can't have.'

'But I did. A month ago. He were alive then, lad; as alive as you and me.'

'My dad?'

'Aye! It was after I went on the run again; they caught me, you see, and they held me overnight in one of their camps. It was one of their roadbuilding camps a ways outside Dover. That's where I saw him.'

'*Engländer!*' The soldier had come to the school gate and was calling impatiently. '*Raus, Engländer!*'

'You saw him?'

'He were sitting in a lorry with a gang of others.'

'What did he say? Tell me what he said. Did you speak to him?'

'Nay, the lorry was only stopped for a minute outside the hut. It moved on before I could speak. But it were him, I'd swear it were. Like I say, that's why I was so took back seeing you and all.'

'Was he . . . He was all right?'

'They put 'em to it on them roads,' the soldier said grimly.

'But he was alive.'

'He was!'

'*Engländer! Raus! Schnell!*'

99

'I'm comin'. Make yourself scarce, lad,' said Yorkie and he grabbed the bucket, splashing water everywhere.

'But why hasn't he told us?' asked Frank desperately. 'Why hasn't anyone told us?'

'This lot play by their own rules, lad. And I doubt your dad's had much time for letter writing. Now, go on, push off before yon Hun turns nasty.' And the soldier hurried away.

'You all right, Frank?' asked Les, coming forward.

'That man tipped water on him,' said Marge Prout, turning off the tap and pointing to Frank's plimsolls. 'He's soaked.'

But Frank didn't care. 'Did you hear him, Les?' he said. 'Did you hear what he said?'

'No. What?'

'Dad's alive; I think my dad's alive.'

'Frank? Where're you going?'

'I've got to tell Nan!'

'Oh, Frank,' said Rose, 'wouldn't it be lovely if it was true!'

'It is true, Rose; he saw him.'

'Who is this Yorkie chap?' said Edie.

'I told you, he's a soldier. Me and dad used to talk to him when we lived in Seabourne.'

'And he said he'd seen Bill?'

'The boy's told us that, girl,' said Nan.

'I know what he's told us, mother. I just don't want anybody getting the wrong end of the stick and getting their hopes up for nothing.'

'You don't want to believe it!' said Frank.

'Frank Tate,' said Edie angrily, 'I hope it's true with all my heart and don't you ever dare think otherwise.'

'Calm down, girl,' said Nan. 'And you too, Frank. Now then, this chap knew Bill and he says he's seen him alive. That's all that matters. Right—you come with me, Frank.'

'Where to, Nan?'

'To see the Firth woman. She'll know the ins and outs of it, who to ask and suchlike. We'll go up there now and tell her what we want.'

'What do we want?'

'I want to know where my son is.'

Warden Firth was on the telephone when the knock came at the door. And she hoped, if she left it long enough, whoever it was would think she was out and go away.

'Knock again, Frank,' said Nan.

'What do you reckon she can do, Nan?' he asked.

'She can write off somewhere. It's answers we want. She always says how she's only doing what she does to help the village—well, let's see her do something to prove it.'

As they waited, the cat, Gargery, appeared from the hedge and stood blinking at them.

'But she's on their side, ain't she?' said Frank quietly.

'There's none so blind, Frank. 'Course, she don't think she is—but like it or not, nobody makes her run their errands and do their spying for them. That's the choice she's made. Here's someone coming now. Don't let her rile you. Just say your piece.'

'I'm afraid it sounds rather fanciful to me, Mrs Tate,' said Betty, when Frank explained what had happened down at The Green.

'I can't help how it sounds,' said Nan. 'I want something done about it.'

'Mrs Tate, if I were to listen to every ridiculous story that was told me—'

'It's not ridiculous,' said Frank. 'Yorkie knew my dad. He'd know if it was him or not. And he saw him. He's not dead. They've made him work on their roads.'

'That's impossible. Apart from convicts I have been assured that all labour is voluntary. I must warn you to think twice before you repeat those sort of rumours. The men working down at The Green were criminals. They are just the sort who would enjoy spreading alarmist and false information.'

'All I want to know is what you're going to do,' said Nan.

'There really is nothing I can do, Mrs Tate.'

'Yes, there is. You could write to somebody.'

'Even if I thought there was an iota of truth in what this man has told you, I simply haven't the time. I don't think anyone understands just how much is involved in ensuring The Day is a success.'

'So you won't help us?'

'I haven't time, Mrs Tate. Perhaps afterwards I might be able to make some enquiries on your behalf but—'

'Dad wouldn't work for the Germans; he wouldn't ever do that!'

'Come on, Frank.'

It wasn't until they'd reached the gate and were hidden behind the big beech hedge that Nan spoke again. 'Damn the woman,' she said. 'Damn and blast her.'

'What are we going to do, Nan?'

'I'm going to have to give it some thought, Frank. But don't you worry, I shall think of something. We ain't beat yet.'

Chapter 8

'Frank?' Colin shook him by the shoulder. 'Frank, wake up!'

Frank rubbed his eyes. 'Col?' he said.

'Wake up.'

'I was dreaming.'

'You were laughing,' said his cousin accusingly.

Frank and his dad: they were both laughing. They were standing on the pavement outside Goodenough's, the department store in the High Street in Seabourne. In the window were the family his dad called the Sunday-Bests. They were sitting in front of their fireplace where the red tissue-paper coals glowed in the grate: Father, with his pipe and newspaper; Mother, with her knitting; and the Children on the rug between them, playing draughts. There was a china cat next to the coal scuttle with a chipped ear.

'You've got to get up.'

'No, I haven't.' Frank pulled the blanket over his head and turned to the wall.

'Yes, you have. Nan wants you. She wants to talk to us. All of us.'

When he got downstairs, Frank found Nan sitting in her chair at the kitchen table. Edie was standing by the sink with her arms folded, and Colin was next to her.

'Right,' said Nan, 'we're all here. Edie, give the boy a drop of tea.'

'You know Saturday is my busy day, mother,' said Edie, filling the cup irritably and placing it in front of Frank. 'What's this all in aid of?'

'I want to tell you what I've decided,' said Nan. 'Colin, keep still!'

'I'm worried, Nan. About getting to Scouts. Sorry, Nan.'

'This is more important than any blessed Scouts. Now listen to me, all of you. The fact is, she ain't going to be a blind bit of help to us.'

'Who?' said Edie.

'Who d'you think? Betty blessed Firth, of course! She can't be bothered. If we're going to find out what's become of Bill we're going to have to find out for ourselves.'

'For heaven's sake, mother,' said Edie, 'what can we do on our own?'

'We can look, that's what. Frank?'

'Yes, Nan.'

'I want you to go to that factory your father used to work at.'

'Bell's, Nan?'

'Don't be so ridiculous, mother.'

'Bell's Precision, Nan?'

'We've got to start from the beginning.' Nan got up and went to the crockery cupboard. She took down a small ornamental teapot, removed the lid and emptied its contents onto the table: a half-crown, two florins, two sixpences, and a threepenny bit.

'That's emergency money,' said Edie.

'That's right,' she said. 'And that's what this is. He can take the fare out of that and go on the mid-morning bus. Will you go, Frank?'

'Yes, Nan,' he said eagerly. ''Course I will.'

'He can't,' said Edie.

'You're to go to that factory and ask them what happened.'

'He can't go all the way to Seabourne on his own.'

'He come all the way here on his own, didn't he?' said Nan.

'Let me go, as well,' said Colin. 'I'll go with you, Frank; I'll help you find your dad.'

'You will not, Colin Worth,' said his mother. 'You've got Scouts this morning. You've got to practise with that flag. No, mother,' she insisted, 'the boy can't go on his own.'

'You go with him, then.'

'Me?' Edie didn't answer at once. Then: 'I couldn't,' she said, 'not on a Saturday.'

'Well, I can't,' said Nan. 'I've got visits as can't be put off. You'll have to go on your own, Frank.'

'No, I won't,' he said, and jumped up from his chair. 'Les can come with me!'

'You two together?' said Edie. 'Don't be so soft.'

'We'd look out for each other.'

'You'd encourage each other into mischief, that's what you'd do.'

'I ain't going to look for mischief, I'm going to look for my dad,' said Frank. 'Please, Nan? Let me take Les with me.'

Les sat on his mattress in the shed and said nothing while Frank explained the plan.

'I'm going to find him, Les; I know I am.'

Les nodded. 'Trouble is, Frank . . . I mean, if—'

'It's all right. She's given me bus fare for us both. And sandwiches. Edie cut loads of sandwiches. Jam. And there's a cheese you can have.'

'It's not that.'

But Frank didn't seem to notice his friend's reticence. 'If we get the half-past ten bus we'll be there by quarter-past twelve.'

Les stood up. 'I've got to talk to Mill,' he said.

'All right.'

'No,' he said, 'you stay here. I shan't be long.'

'Do what?' said Mill, putting down the dishcloth and looking at him in disbelief. 'Les Gill, you want your head read!'

'He's going looking for his dad.'

'You ain't never thinking of going with him, are you?'

'He asked me to.'

'And have you said you would?'

Les shrugged.

'For gawd's sake, Les! It'd be asking for trouble. What if the police was to stop you?'

'The ones at the checkpoint stop me every day. Nobody ain't ever said anything.'

'That's here, ennit? That's not somewhere like Seabourne.'

'There'll be crowds of people, Mill. They ain't going to pick on me particular.'

'And what if they do? Ain't that just the sort of place they'd have the information on us?'

'How d'you mean?'

'Use your common, Les, do! The police and the Jerries pass it on to each other, don't they.' She glanced out into the yard and into the passageway beyond the kitchen to make sure they weren't overheard. 'Look,' she said, 'if them Crockers reported us, and you can bet they have, there'll be a warrant out for us. And our descriptions and everything. Have you thought of that?'

'Yes.'

'Well, then!'

Les shook his head. 'He's my pal, Mill. I can't let him down. I can't do that.'

'Tell him, then. Tell him what happened. If he knew that and he was your pal he wouldn't expect you to go with him.'

Les was silent for a moment. Then: 'Nah,' he said, 'I can't.'

'You just want to go, that's what it is,' said Mill. 'You ain't listened to a blind word I've said.'

'I have, Mill.'

'No, you ain't.'

They stood facing each other across the kitchen.

'I got to go,' he said.

'Well, I can't stop you,' she said.

'I'll keep me head down, Mill,' he said. 'Like we agreed. You know that. I promise.'

But she wasn't listening. She had turned away and was busy clattering dirty plates noisily from the draining-board into the sink.

'Where's your bucket and spade?' laughed the bus conductor when Frank asked for two returns, please. Halves. All the way.

Once they had settled in their seats the two boys fell silent: Les, hunched beside the window; and Frank occupied with his own thoughts, as he watched the countryside slip by. Memories. Mostly memories. Of that other journey. Of the last time he'd come that way. When he'd thought he was leaving Seabourne for ever.

The White Horse Inn had been full of soldiers. As he went down the stairs, there was furniture stacked on all the landings. Mr Burford was standing outside at the foot of the steps. Despite the sunshine, he was wearing his big tweed overcoat. He was cradling his antique clock and his attaché case of photographs in his arms. There were two suitcases on the pavement beside him; and the picture of Ivor Novello from over his mantelpiece. 'The White Horse is my home,' he was pleading. 'My dear mother was married from this house.' But the German officer was taking no notice. Burford began to cry. 'Please let me stay? You must. It's only me.' He looked up and pointed to the steps where Frank was standing. 'He's not with me. The boy is nothing to do with me. Tell them, Frank, please! Tell them you're not mine. Tell them it's only me!'

Today the bus would be at the bus station in Kilgarriff Street in less than two hours. But today the road across the Downs was empty; there were no columns of weary refugees traipsing behind their carts and prams; or speeding convoys of troop-carriers racing inland to victory. How quickly things changed. That was the war; the war made things happen quickly. Things you couldn't imagine being so one moment were a fact the next. He had come down this road the last time sure he would never see his dad again. Now . . .

'There's the sea!' Frank pointed as they came over the hill. 'See it shining?'

'Are we nearly there, then?'

'Yes, it's not far now.' Frank settled back in his seat. 'Here,' he said, 'you never told me what Mill said; you know, when you told her where we were going. What did she say? Said it was stupid, did she?'

'You know Mill.'

'Did she try and stop you coming?'

'Why would she want to do that?'

'I only wondered. She's always going on about keeping our heads down and everything and not doing anything that might—What's the matter?'

Les had turned away and was looking out of the window. 'We've stopped,' he said.

The bus had pulled up at the junction with the main road, and was being held there by a motorcycle outrider. Along the road stretched a convoy of guns and tanks moving slowly in the direction of the coast.

'What's the betting they're on their way to Russia?' said Frank. 'Remember the films the other night?' But Les wasn't listening. He was watching the soldier from the motorcycle's sidecar, who had got out to stretch his legs and was walking along the side of the bus. The soldier looked up, saw Les watching, and stared back at him.

Les looked away. 'How far is it now?' he said.

'I told you, not far,' said Frank. And got up. 'I'm going to ask the conductor to put us off near Bell's Precision.'

The conductor was rolling a cigarette while he and the driver waited for the convoy to pass. 'Bell's?' he said, and ran the tip of his tongue along the gummed edge of the cigarette-paper. 'I thought you was on your way to the sea.'

'No. I'm going to find my dad,' said Frank.

108

'Work there, does he?'

'He used to. We don't know where he is now. But I'm going to ask them.'

The conductor and the driver glanced at each other. 'Worked at Bell's?' said the conductor. 'The old Bell's Precision?'

'Yes.'

'I'll give you a shout when we're there.'

When the shout came, Frank grabbed Les and they stumbled up the gangway.

'Get a move on,' said the conductor. 'I'm late as it is.'

They got down and the bus drew away leaving them on the pavement opposite the factory gate.

'Is this it?' asked Les.

'I think so,' said Frank doubtfully. 'I don't understand.'

On the signboard above the entrance to the factory were the words:

DEUTSCHER
WERKZEUGMASCHINENBAU

They crossed the road and stood looking up at the sign. A man in overalls came out of the hut inside the gate. 'Oi!' he called. 'Don't hang about there. There's vehicles in and out all the time. Go on, hop it!'

'Isn't this Bell's any more?' said Frank.

'What do you think that says?' said the man, pointing to the sign.

'But it used to be Bell's.' The man's overalls smelt of oil, the way his dad's used to. 'This was Bell's Precision,' said Frank.

A lorry bearing Wehrmacht military insignia and registration plates drew out of the yard and turned away along the road. Its cargo was draped in heavy tarpaulin sheets.

'My dad worked here.'

'When was that?' asked the man.

'Before,' said Frank. 'You know, before the Jerries came. I've come to look for him.'

'I can't help you there,' said the man. 'They only took me on recently.'

'He was here the night they came,' said Frank. 'But we don't know where he is now.'

The man looked over his shoulder towards the factory. Then said quietly, 'Skilled man, was he, your dad?'

'They sent him to lots of factories.'

'Only I know there was some—you know, the skilled ones—who stayed on. But there was a few—' The gatekeeper broke off as another lorry came in through the gates and began to sound its horn impatiently. He hurried across and, collecting some papers from the driver, directed him to the buildings on the other side of the yard; then he took the papers with him and went back into his hut.

By the time Frank reached the hut the gatekeeper had picked up the telephone and was dialling.

'What were you going to say?' said Frank. 'About the skilled men?'

'Look, I don't know all the ins and outs of it; I wasn't here,' he said. 'You go through channels, that's your best bet. Channels. They'll have records, see? They've got records of everything. Very fond of lists, the Germans.' He began to shuffle through the documents the driver had handed him, as someone answered the phone at the other end. 'Stores?' he said.

'Channels?' said Frank desperately.

The man put his hand over the mouthpiece. 'Try the Town Hall,' he said. 'And don't say I told you.'

As they crossed the road and headed into town, Les said, 'What did they make—you know, when your dad worked there?'

'Tools,' said Frank.

'What, hammers and screwdrivers?'

'No—machine tools. For making planes and things for the war.'

There was bunting and flags strung across the High Street, and Hitler's picture hung in several shop

110

windows. The windows themselves were not very full; and there were queues at most of the shop doors. A military band was playing somewhere in the direction of the pier; and the streets were full of German soldiers, standing at corners or strolling together. Some had girls with them, arm in arm, laughing; a group of them had taken possession of the seats underneath the clock in the Civic Gardens, where, before the war, the trippers used to sit eating fish and chips.

'That's Goodenough's over there,' said Frank, as they crossed The Circus. 'They used to sell everything.'

'Is it far to the Town Hall?'

'No, it's only round the corner. Les!'

But Frank's warning came too late. Les walked straight into the three soldiers who stepped from the doorway of The Welcome Glass. They weren't drunk, but he could smell the beer as the one on the end leaned forward and took him by the shoulder.

'You must beg my pardon, I think,' said the soldier.

'I didn't see you,' stammered Les.

'*Matthias?*' The other two had walked on along the pavement. '*Matthias,*' they called, '*laß' das Kind in Ruhe! Komm schnell!*'

'*Moment!*' the soldier replied. He grinned at Les. 'I have,' he said, 'no hard feelings. This is correct?' He fumbled in the pocket of his tunic and produced a bar of chocolate. 'For you,' he said. 'What is your name? Tell me your name.'

Les shook his head.

The soldier frowned. Then his eyes widened knowingly. 'So!' he said. And he winked. 'Not chocolate.' He reached into his pocket again and this time brought out a packet of cigarettes. 'Better for you?' He grinned and tucked the packet into Les's shirt. 'What do you say to me?'

And Frank remembered what his cousin Rose had said. Or something that sounded like it. 'Off,' he said, 'off weedersane!'

'*Auf Wiedersehn!*' The soldier laughed: '*Oh, sehr gut! Der spricht gut Deutsch*,' he observed to his companions. He held out his hand to Frank. 'You must shake my hand now,' he said.

Les watched helplessly. It seemed that Frank's hand would never move from his side. But finally and slowly it did, and the soldier took it and shook it heartily.

'*Genau so* "English gentlemen"', yes? No hard feelings?' he said. '*Auf Wiedersehn!*' And he and his companions went off along the pavement.

Frank rubbed his hand angrily on his shirt.

'Come on!' said Les, pulling him away. 'Time's getting on.'

There was a queue outside the Town Hall; and at the top of the steps next to the entrance a soldier was sitting at a table checking people's identity cards.

'I'd better wait here,' said Les. 'You know, till you come out.'

'But I don't know how long it'll take,' said Frank.

'I'd rather be outside,' said Les. 'I feel a bit sick. It was being on the bus, I expect. I'll wait on the steps.'

'All right.'

When Frank's turn came he tried to explain to the soldier why he was there, but the soldier simply handed him a piece of paper with a number on it. 'Missing Persons,' he said. 'You must go to that room.' And beckoned the next person to the table.

The door was at the end of a long, marbled corridor. Frank knocked and waited. It was opened by a tall woman with spectacles.

'Yes?' she said.

Beyond her, the windowless room was lined with shelves on which there were files and bundles of documents. A man sat at a table in the middle of the room and there was a smaller table with a typewriter on it nearby. The man wasn't wearing a uniform but Frank was sure he was a Jerry.

'What is it you want?' said the woman.

112

'Missing Persons,' said Frank.

'That's right,' she said, and started back towards the shelves. 'Missing when?'

'Last year,' he said. He glanced at the German but he didn't appear to be listening. 'You know, about the time they came.'

'In the Seabourne area?' Frank nodded. The woman reached up and pulled out one of the files. 'Name?' she said.

'Tate. Bill Tate. William Thomas Tate.' He hesitated; he had never called his dad that before. 'That was what it was on his Identity Card,' he said. 'He's my dad.'

'Military?'

'No.'

The woman removed a sheet of paper from the file. She ran her finger down it. 'No,' she said, 'there's no one of that name here. Here, see for yourself; I know people like to.'

He took it from her. At the top it said:

CIVILIAN CASUALTIES; SEABOURNE and AREA, September to October 1940.

Beneath the headings: DEAD and WOUNDED, were two short columns of closely typed names in alphabetical order.

'He's not here,' said Frank.

'That's good news, isn't it?' said the woman.

'Is it?'

'Oh, yes,' she said. 'It usually means they're alive.'

'But he is alive,' said Frank.

The woman looked at him. 'Then what are you doing here?'

'Because he's still missing. I think he was taken prisoner.'

'You said he was a civilian.'

'He is. He was working at the factory, you see. Actually he was fire-watching that night.'

The German at the table looked up. 'Which factory?' he said.

'Bell's,' said Frank. 'Bell's Precision. It's called something different now. That's where he worked. I just want to know what happened to him.'

The German stood up. 'Crucial personnel at the firm formerly known as Bell's Precision were offered the choice of continuing their employment. Those who refused were redeployed in essential work elsewhere.'

'Where? What sort of work?'

'Essential work.'

'Building roads? That's where he was seen.'

'The information you require is not held in this office. You must enquire from the Organization Todt.' He looked at his watch. 'We are closing now.'

'Closing?'

'It's Saturday,' said the woman. 'We close at one o'clock.'

'If you please, Frau Collier?' The man gestured towards the door.

The woman took Frank's arm and led him out into the corridor. 'You mustn't give up,' she whispered. 'The O.T. are the ones you want.'

'What's that?'

'The Organization Todt. Get your Blockwarden to write to them. That's the best. Do it through your Blockwarden.'

'But that's why I'm here.'

'Frau Collier, the door, please!'

'Good luck,' she said, and disappeared back into the room.

Outside the entrance the soldier was packing up his table. The queue had dispersed and the only ones left were an elderly man and woman who stood shaking their heads over some forms. There were shoppers hurrying past in the street below; and two men in trilby hats and raincoats standing on the steps watching them. But of Les there was no sign at all.

Chapter 9

Where? Where was Les?

Frank was about to ask the two men in raincoats if they'd seen the boy who had been sitting on the steps, but when he heard them speaking German to each other he changed his mind. He ran down into the street and looked anxiously this way and that. Where? Where would Les go? Halfway along the row of shops opposite the Town Hall, a bomb or shell had opened up a gap right through to the High Street. The buildings on either side were untouched, and on the open ground between them a makeshift market was in progress.

Near the pavement a man with a card-table was selling loose cigarettes; and next to him, a woman was sitting in a wicker chair with a suitcase full of books in front of her. There were one or two stalls and some trestle tables; but mostly people with things to offer stood holding them up in front of them: a vase, a watch, a pair of smart shoes. He passed an elderly man who held open a box lined with velvet on which was displayed an elegant dinner service. The busiest people were those selling vegetables, potatoes and cabbage and onions; and the woman with the rail of second-hand clothes. The buildings on either side of the site had been shored up with timber, and high on one wall he could see a fireplace; there was wallpaper above it and you could see the light patch where the mirror had once hung. He tried to remember the shops that had been there. But the bomb, or whatever it was, had transformed it so completely that it was almost

115

impossible to imagine the site had ever been anything other than a ruin. No—Booth's! That was it! It had been Booth's Reliable Footwear! His dad had bought him some plimsolls there not long after they'd first come to Seabourne. And the other one, the one that looked out on to the High Street, had been the Clifton! The Clifton Tea and Coffee Rooms, where the shoppers had been served their plates of fancy cakes by waitresses in brown and white uniforms.

'Frank?'

He turned, and was relieved to see Les coming through the crowd. 'Les! Les, where have you been?'

'I saw you come out the Town Hall,' said Les.

'You said you'd wait outside.'

'I know. I couldn't help it. It was them two on the steps, they was watching me.'

'What?'

'They was stopping people; you know, asking them questions. I think they must have been Gestapo. I had to make meself scarce.'

'Why? Why did you just push off like that?'

'I had to.'

'But you weren't doing anything wrong.'

'I told you, they was . . . you know, watching me.'

'But you were only sitting on the steps,' insisted Frank. 'They weren't going to arrest you for sitting on the steps, were they?'

'I don't know.' They stood facing each other, each one waiting for the other to speak. Finally, Les said, 'Look, I promised Mill, didn't I?'

'Promised Mill what?'

'To keep out of trouble.'

'You weren't in any trouble, Les.'

'What will you give me? For them both?' A tall boy about their own age with a pale, drawn face thrust two packets of cigarette cards at them. 'It's the County Cricketers Series,' he said, 'Sussex and Hampshire, the complete sets. None missing. Honestly. Half a crown?'

'We haven't got any money,' said Frank.

'Give me two shillings, then.' The boy's pullover was dirty and darned in several places, but his voice was what Les called 'pound-note-ish'.

'I told you,' said Frank, 'we haven't got any money.'

'I can't take less than two shillings.'

'I told you—'

'Don't you like cricket?'

All the time he was speaking the boy's eyes had never stopped watching the crowd; and seeing a man and a boy stop to look at the clothes-rail, he turned away quickly and started in their direction.

Frank turned back to Les. 'Les?'

'What?'

'Les, I don't understand—you weren't in any trouble.'

'I was, Frank.' Les shook his head. 'You don't understand,' he said, and sat down on what remained of a wall. 'I promised Mill.'

'Promised her what?'

'She didn't want me to come.'

'But you said . . . ' Frank sat down next to him. 'Why not?'

'I ought to have told you. That's what she said; she said if I'd have told you . . .   The thing is . . . Look, remember what I told you about the Crockers, the ones me and Mill was billeted with?'

'The ones with the sweet shop? The ones who were killed by the shell?'

'There weren't no shell,' said Les.

'But you said—'

'I know. But there weren't no shell. Or nothing. We run away from 'em. It was her, see—Dot Crocker; she used to knock Mill about. And Bert, he was bevvied a lot of the time and he just let her. And Mill, she wouldn't tell nobody about it. I told her to, lots of times, but she wouldn't.'

'Why not?'

'She reckoned if she did the ones in charge would split us up. So she went on getting bashed.'

'So you ran away?'

'No, she wouldn't do that neither. She said she had to be grown-up about it. That's what she always says. You know, about her being grown-up and that. That's why she's so bossy and likes to have a fag stuck in her mouth. She said that if we was caught they'd still split us up. And she wasn't having that. But I used to think about it all the time; I used to try and think of ways of getting her away from them. Then one afternoon, I was sitting in the shop—Bert was down at the Fusilier and Dot was upstairs; she'd sent Mill out to keep a place in a queue for her, she was like that—I was just sitting there, in the shop, and it come to me. I opened the till and took ten bob out. It was easy. Then I went and put me and Mill's stuff into a couple of big bags and went and looked for her. When I found her I told her what I'd done. I told her how Bert would have come back by now and how I was a thief and we'd have to run away or the coppers would be after me.'

'What did she say?'

'Oh, she led off at me alarming—you know Mill. But I think she was glad really. I mean, she didn't hang about arguing—well, not for long; she just picked up her bag and started walking there and then. We was on the road a month and more, I think.'

'Till Vera Thrale took you in.'

'Yeah. Mill reckoned Shevington was the sort of place where they wouldn't be looking for us. It is. But she still worries. She worries about questions being asked and the police sending out our descriptions and that. That's why she makes me keep me head down. That's why I have to keep out of trouble; any sort of trouble. That's why she didn't want me coming here.'

'But you still came.'

'You asked me to.'

'Les, you should have told me before.'

'Why? There ain't nothing anybody can do about it.'

''Course, there is. 'Cos you haven't done anything.'

'Leave off, Frank. What did I just tell you?'

'Les, hundreds of kids must have run away like that. Thousands. The police and the Germans don't go round looking for them. They don't care. They've got the Resistance and saboteurs to catch. They aren't going to bother with you and Mill, Les. Les, they're not!'

'I nicked that ten bob and all though, didn't I!'

'I'm telling you, Les, the Gestapo aren't looking for you over ten bob.'

'That's what Mill thinks.'

'She's wrong.'

'You tell her that,' said Les resignedly.

They sat for a while and watched the crowd drifting by; and saw the boy with the cigarette cards go past holding a cabbage under his arm. From somewhere down by the pier the sound of a military band came drifting up the High Street.

'So what did they say at the Town Hall?' said Les.

'He wasn't killed. They showed me the list.'

'That's good news then, ennit?'

'I know. But there's something funny about it.'

'How d'you mean?'

'There was a German in the room with all the papers, and when he heard that Dad had worked at Bell's Precision . . . I don't know, he was just funny about it, that's all.'

'What're you going to do?'

'Go back and tell Nan. We've got to write to some Department or the other: the O.T. We'll have to have another go at Betty Firth. But you know what a cow she is. The next bus goes at two o'clock. I suppose we'd better go to the bus station and wait.'

'What, now?' said Les. 'But ain't we going to . . . you know, have a look round?'

'What do you mean?'

'You know, where you used to live? That sort of thing?'

119

'We'd have to go down to the seafront, wouldn't we?'

Les shrugged. 'I just thought, you know . . . I just thought you might want to go and see it, that's all.'

'I do. But if we went down there . . . Look, if we went down there you'd just be looking out for policemen all the time, wouldn't you? Come on. We'll go to the bus station.'

'No, wait!' Les scrambled to his feet. 'I wouldn't, Frank; I wouldn't be looking for coppers all the time. What I mean is . . . What you said and that . . . I mean, I mean when you think about it, they ain't no more likely to stop me than anyone else, are they? Not really.'

'You mean you believe me, then?'

Les shrugged. 'It don't seem fair, that's all. Now we're here and that. And I could still keep me head down, couldn't I?'

'All right! We'll go and see The White Horse Inn. We've got time for that before the bus goes. I'll tell you what we'll do—we won't go along the front; I'll take you the short-cut the other side of the High Street instead.'

'Eh? No, don't do that,' said Les quickly. 'I mean . . . well, if we was to go along the seafront we could eat them sandwiches, couldn't we?'

Frank look puzzled. 'Yes,' he said.

'You know—by the sea and that,' said Les. 'Only . . . truth is, Frank . . . '

'What's the matter?'

'I ain't never seen it.'

'Seen what?'

'The sea.'

'What—never?' Les shook his head. 'Everybody ought to see the sea, Les.'

'And it ain't far, is it?'

'Bottom of the High Street. Come on.'

They could see all the way to the horizon where a pale line of sunlight glittered coldly on the grey water. There was a stiffish wind blowing and the tide was advancing in long diagonals of white-topped waves which broke noisily along the deserted tideline. In several places there were still deep craters in the pebbles where shells had landed; and against the wall of the Prom was piled the splintered remains of a small fishing boat, its lobster pots tangled beside it.

'This bay was full of warships,' said Frank, as they leaned against the railings eating the sandwiches Edie had prepared. 'You should have heard the row the guns made. I was in the cellar and I couldn't hear for days.'

'How far does it go?'

'France is over there. You can't see it. They say you can at Dover; but not here, it's too far.'

'Is it always so rough?'

'In winter it used to come right up over these railings.'

''Struth!' said Les. 'I wouldn't mind seeing that.'

'This is where Yorkie used to come with his patrol— you know, the soldier who told me about Dad. This is where we used to talk to him.'

Up in the town the clock in the Civic Gardens sounded the half hour. Frank finished his sandwich. 'We ought to get on,' he said. 'The White Horse Inn is only just along the seafront but we haven't got very much time.'

'Right ho,' said Les. 'Good sandwiches, them.'

'Yes,' said Frank. 'Edie must have gone a bit barmy; she ain't usually so generous.'

'Seabourne got off light, didn't it?' Les observed, as they moved on along the Prom. 'Considerin' how they landed here.'

'That's what they wanted it for—to land. It was the guns up on the Downs they were firing at. 'Course, some shells hit the town, like where that market is now—yes, and over there.' He pointed across the road to the row of small hotels and guest houses; the one one from the end had the dark marks of fire around its windows, and inside you could see scorched rafters and fallen ceilings. 'That was the Ivanhoe,' said Frank. 'It was quite posh. It's the only place on the seafront that was really badly damaged.'

'Frank?'

'What?'

'Who's that?' Les had stopped and was pointing to a figure walking along in front of them: a man in a light-coloured raincoat with his collar turned up against the wind, clutching his cap to his head and carrying a large shopping basket. 'Ain't there something about him?'

'I don't know. Is there?'

'Blimey!' said Les. 'Yes, there is! I'll tell you what it is and all. You know who that is, don't you? It's the Toff!'

'Don't be daft.'

'It is, Frank. It is; it's old Sims!'

The man stopped, put on his spectacles, and looked hard at a piece of paper he pulled from his pocket. Then he looked back along the Prom.

''Struth,' said Frank, 'it is him! What's he doing here?'

'Getting lost by the look of it.'

'No, look.'

The teacher thrust the paper back in his pocket, and stepped off the pavement. The oncoming lorry swerved and the driver called out but Sims didn't seem to notice and carried on to the other side of the road.

'He shouldn't be out on his own,' said Les.

'I'll say he shouldn't.' Frank laughed. 'Here, tell you what, Les,' he said, 'why don't me and you keep an eye on him?'

'What, follow him?'

'Yes. What d'you say?'

'Lively, then!'

Sims was walking quickly. He took the first turning back towards the town and then turned into Balmoral Street, the street of houses behind the seafront hotels. When he reached the far end, where it met the Bowling

Green, he stopped and consulted his piece of paper again. On the town side of the Green stood the Quadrant, a crescent of elegant three-storey houses with wrought-iron balconies and basements below the level of the pavement. Sims crossed the road and made his way slowly from house to house, looking up at the numbers on the doors. He didn't stop until he reached the house at the far end. There he consulted his piece of paper once more, then made his way tentatively down the steps into the basement.

'What do you think he's doing?' said Frank.

'With that basket,' said Les, 'and looking so shifty? Obvious, ennit.'

'What d'you mean?'

'He's come shopping.'

'Shopping?'

'Black market,' said Les conclusively, 'that's what it is. You mark my words.'

'What, the Toff? Never?'

'Fags, that's what Bert Crocker used to have under the counter. And there was a bloke down the road used to do petrol. But he got caught.'

'The police?'

'No, some other crooks. They smashed his shop up.'

'Fancy old Sims knowing . . .' Frank shook his head.

'Knowing what?'

'Knowing crooks; and knowing where to go and everything.'

'Bert Crocker used to say it wasn't him was the crook 'cos it was the Jerries who was crooks,' said Les. 'We going to wait and see him come out?'

'No,' said Frank, 'we haven't got time. Come on, let's go and see The White Horse. We can cut across the Green.'

The Municipal Bowling Green had been neglected; the once smooth surface was overgrown and stained with patches of dark moss and weeds. It was deserted; except for a man sitting in the shelter where the bowlers used to keep out of the rain, and a second man sitting on a bench opposite reading a newspaper.

'This is where I saw the dead body,' said Frank. 'Remember me telling you about that? Over there in the gully. He'd been hit by a pebble. Les?'

But Les wasn't listening; he had stopped and was looking across towards the shelter. The man sitting there had climbed up on to the seat and was peering over the privet hedge towards the Quadrant. Then, as Sims's head appeared coming back up the basement steps, he jumped down again quickly. The teacher paused when he reached the pavement, looked up and down the street, and then set off back the way he had come. The man in the shelter signalled to the man with the newspaper, who got up and hurried across to him. The two of them spoke briefly and then went out through the gate and began to follow Sims down the street.

'They're going after him,' said Les.

'Think it's the police?' said Frank.

'It might be other crooks. We ought to tell him.'

'I know how we can head him off. Come on!'

Between the hotels and the houses that faced Balmoral Street was an alley which gave access to their backyards. They ran along it until they reached the end, where they waited for Sims to appear and turn down towards the seafront. But when he did appear, instead of turning, he walked straight on and continued along the next street. His pursuers, it seemed, were keeping their distance and Frank and Les had time to cross the road and run on along the alley on the other side. When they reached the end they waited again. This time Sims turned the corner and began to head back towards the sea. But then he seemed to realize this wasn't the street he'd come up and stopped to take out his piece of paper. Frank ran out. 'Quick, sir,' he said, 'they're after you.' And grabbing him by the sleeve, he dragged him into the alley.

'Tate?' Peter Sims was too surprised to do anything

but blink. 'Is that you, Tate? Good Lord, Gill?' he said, when he saw Les waiting by one of the yard doors.

'In here, sir,' said Les. 'We can hide inside.'

'But why? What—'

'I told you, sir,' said Frank. 'There's people following you.'

They bundled him past the rusting dustbins and in through the back door of the building. Inside was a warren of corridors and doors opening on to rooms charred and blackened by fire and smoke. A stairway rose immediately in front of them and they hurried up it until they reached the first floor landing and a window overlooking the yard. Frank put his finger to his lips and they flattened themselves out of sight against the wall. Almost at once there was the sound of rapid footsteps and of doors being thrown open all along the alley. Someone ran into the yard below, they heard him curse as his feet crunched on the broken glass; but then, as they held their breaths, a voice called, 'Leave it, Terry! He must have gone back along the Prom. Quick!' The footsteps crunched away; and then there was silence. They waited, not daring to move. They could hear the band playing in the distance. Finally, Frank leaned forward and looked out into the alley.

'They've gone,' he said.

'Dear heavens!' Sims took out a handkerchief and wiped his forehead; he was sweating. 'I had no idea that anyone was following me.'

'They was watching the house,' said Les, 'the one you went into.'

'We saw them,' said Frank. 'So we thought we'd better tell you.'

'But what are you boys doing here?'

'I used to live here,' said Frank. 'Not here; this was the Ivanhoe,' he gestured back into the darkened building. 'It was a posh hotel. I used to live further along the seafront.'

'This is all very unfortunate,' said Sims.

'It's all right, sir, you can trust us.'

'The shopping,' said Les, and winked.

'The fact of the matter is,' said Sims, 'I have to get back to the bus station, rather urgently.'

'That's where we're going,' said Frank. 'You can come with us.'

'No, Tate. No, that isn't possible. I couldn't endanger you.'

'But I know all the quick ways, sir. I told you. I used to live here.'

'Even so. Perhaps if you were to explain them to me I—'

'You'd never find the way.'

'Them two out there would find you first,' said Les.

Peter Sims looked down at the yard and the maze of streets beyond the alley. 'I seem to have very little choice,' he said.

'First thing to do,' said Les, 'is to take off your hat and coat.'

'My hat and coat?'

'Because they're looking for someone in a hat and coat, ain't they? Roll them up and put them in your basket.'

'Very well.'

'And put your glasses on,' said Les.

'Yes, my spectacles. I took them off as a precaution,' said Sims. 'I was advised to take precautions. But it made life rather difficult. I can't see terribly well without them.'

'What we got to do is split up. Frank, you go in front. And me and Mr Sims will follow you. All right, sir?'

'You're very resourceful, Gill,' said Sims. 'I'm most grateful.'

'And let me take the basket,' said Frank. 'They're not looking for a boy with a basket, are they?'

'No,' said Sims quickly. 'No, I can't do that. You see . . . Look here, it's all rather difficult to explain but I'm not supposed to let it out of my sight.'

The sound of the clock striking the quarter turned them all towards the window.

'We're going to have to shift,' said Les. 'That bus goes at two.'

Chapter 10

Behind the Promenade was a maze of narrow streets and alleyways; and whenever Frank turned out of sight, Les and Mr Sims quickened their pace anxiously. But each time, when they reached the corner, he was there, hurrying along on the other side. There were children playing in the road and shoppers going by; in one street a woman was on her knees scrubbing her front step and in another a man and a small girl were watering a window-box filled with brightly coloured flowers. No one seemed to take any particular notice of the boy and the nervous-looking man with the shopping basket.

At the corner of Medlar Street Frank risked a quick glance over his shoulder: they were still there. The main thing was to go quickly and to keep an eye out for Sims's pursuers: the crooks. Frank was convinced now that that was what they were: the sort of shady characters he'd seen in films about the underworld, men who worked for bookmakers or smugglers. After all, the black market was just like smuggling. The ones in the olden days, the ones who wore three-cornered hats, had been after French brandy and tobacco. But now the black market . . . What was it Les had said? Fags and petrol. Yes. But when he thought about it, Frank couldn't remember ever seeing Sims smoking; and he didn't have a car. So if it wasn't like Les said, then what was it the teacher had concealed in his basket?

'Do you think it's much further?' said Sims, as they saw Frank turn out of sight yet again. He fumbled in his top pocket and took out his watch. 'We have four minutes before the bus leaves.'

'Frank'll get us there,' Les assured him. 'He knows this place like the back of his hand.'

'I should never have involved you boys in this.'

'Don't make no odds, sir,' said Les, 'we was going for the bus anyway.' And if it comes to it, he thought, looking at the basket clasped tightly in the teacher's hand, all we've got to do is dump it quick. Over a wall or somewhere. The lucky perisher who found it would think it was Christmas.

As Frank crossed the High Street, the military band which had been playing on the Promenade swung into view. The bandmaster strutted proudly in front, one hand on his hip and the other beating time with a baton, which dipped and rose as they marched. Their uniforms were dull and grey, but the way they marched, with such precision, and the music they played, so sure of itself, turned heads and made people stand to watch them go by.

The bus station was a large enclosed yard with a curved roof of corrugated metal. In the middle of the yard was an island where there was a Ticket Office and a Waiting Room with a tea-stall outside. The bus stops were situated around the edge of the island, and when Frank arrived there were queues at all of them and three buses waiting. The one opposite the Ticket Office had 'Shevington' displayed on its destination board, and the driver was already in his seat. He ran across to where the conductor was leaning against the bonnet with a mug of tea in his hand.

'Is this the one goes at two o'clock?' he asked.

'That's right,' the conductor replied, looking up at the clock on the wall of the Ticket Office. It was two minutes to two. 'I'd get aboard if I were you.' He tipped the dregs from his mug onto the roadway and walked away towards the tea-stall.

Frank looked towards the entrance. Where were they?

They shouldn't have been so far behind him, should they? A car swept into the yard and pulled up in front of the Waiting Room. Out of it jumped the crook who'd been reading the newspaper on the Bowling Green. And with him was someone else Frank recognized—it was one of the men in raincoats from the Town Hall steps: the Gestapo agent. They stood talking together, looking across at the waiting queues. If Sims and Les arrived now they would walk right into them. And if they didn't, the bus would certainly go without them. Where were they?

The policeman on duty at The Circus had stepped into the road and held up his hand to stop anyone crossing until the band had gone by. Les and Mr Sims had been forced to wait at the pavement's edge while Frank plunged into the crowd on the other side and disappeared around the corner. The moment the last bandsman had passed, and despite the shout from the policeman, they rushed across the road.

'There it is, sir!' said Les, as they turned into Kilgarriff Street and saw the Downways Bus Company sign above the entrance. 'Come on!'

The clock was showing two o'clock as they ran into the yard. It was Les who saw them first: the Gestapo agent and the other one were outside the Waiting Room, staring in through the window. They had only to look across the yard and that would be that.

The bus conductor had returned his mug and was walking back from the tea-stall. The driver waved and started the engine. Frank watched helplessly. Les and Sims were standing in full view; they didn't seem able to move. Then, suddenly, there was a shout and everyone turned. The owner of the tea-stall came running out from behind the counter shaking his fist and shouting at a man in a shabby overcoat who was standing in front of the stall stuffing something into his mouth.

'I've warned you,' he shouted. 'It's every blessed day! You're a blasted thief! That's what you are!' The stall-holder turned and addressed the Gestapo man and his companion. 'Every blessed day. And you lot don't do a damn thing about it. You're supposed to be the police, aren't you?' The Gestapo man waved him away; but he wouldn't be put off. 'Well, aren't you? What are you going to do about it?'

The man in the overcoat made no attempt to escape but stood with his arms at his sides and his head bowed. Then, while the stall-holder continued to argue with the Gestapo agent, he looked up, threw back his head, and started to sing:

'We'll gather lilacs in the spring again,

And walk together down an English lane . . . '

People began to laugh. But Frank could only stare in disbelief. The man was singing at the top of his voice now:

'Until our hearts have learned to sing again,

When you come home once more.'

It was—it was the song Mr Burford always used to sing. And that was the old tweed overcoat he'd always worn. He recognized it now. But it couldn't be—it couldn't be Gordon Burford, could it?

'Now, sir,' hissed Les. 'It's our only chance!'

A bus which had just arrived at the entrance turned in from the street and began to move slowly across the yard. Keeping it between them and the island, Les and Sims reached the Shevington stop and slipped along the side of the bus to where Frank was waiting.

'Quick, Frank!' said Les desperately. And pushed Sims up the steps.

Frank didn't move. He couldn't. More people were laughing now. And the Gestapo agent and his companion were bundling Burford away.

'Never seen "Poor Gordon" before?' said the conductor and laughed. 'Always hanging about the bus station. He steals cakes, sandwiches, anything he can get down before he's caught. Poor devil! Up you get now, sonny. Hold very tight, please!' he called, and rang the bell.

The bus waited briefly before moving out into the street. Through the back window Frank saw that they had spreadeagled Gordon Burford on the bonnet of the car and were punching him and pulling him this way and that. He was still singing. Or he might have been screaming.

It wasn't until they were well clear of the town that Les said, 'You all right, sir?'

Sims nodded. 'Yes, thank you, Gill.'

'I reckon that loony saved our bacon, don't you, Frank? Frank? You all right?'

'It was him,' said Frank quietly. 'That was Mr Burford.'

'Who?'

'From The White Horse Inn. That was Mr Burford, Les.'

'Blimey, Frank! But he was . . . '

'I didn't recognize him.'

'Did you know that man?' asked Sims.

'Yes, sir; me and my dad used to live in his house.'

'In his house?'

So Frank told him about The White Horse Inn, and his dad, and what he and Les had been doing in Seabourne that afternoon; about his visit to the Town Hall and what had happened there. The teacher sat, the basket on his knees, nodding from time to time, but it was difficult to tell whether he was really listening.

The bus crossed the coast road and climbed slowly to the top of the Downs. They had passed the summit and were descending the hill on the Shevington side when, without any warning, the driver stamped hard on the brakes and everyone on board was thrown forwards out of their seats. There were shouts and laughter, and the driver called out his apologies, pointing to a pair of sheep who had wandered off the verge and into the road, and who were taking their time going back despite repeated blasts of his horn. Sitting side by side on the back seat, Les, Frank, and Mr Sims had been thrown to the floor. The shock of the fall had dislodged Sims's raincoat from the top of the basket. As Frank stooped to pick it up, he saw that the covering cloth had slipped to one side and the contents of the basket could now be seen quite plainly. Onions . . . large, red onions! Eight? Ten? More! He tried to catch Les's attention but Les was looking out of the window at the sheep, who were returning casually to the grass beside the road. He handed Sims his mac.

'Thank you, Tate,' said the teacher, replacing it on top of the basket, unaware that Frank had glimpsed the contraband in the bottom.

Onions! Frank couldn't believe it. Yes, onions! All that fuss, all that trouble, for a few old onions! And he laughed.

'Are you all right, Tate?'

'Yes, sir,' he said. 'I was just thinking that's all.' Thinking how Les would laugh too when he told him.

At each place the bus stopped more people got off and by the time they reached the turning for Shevington, Frank, Les, and Mr Sims had the back of the bus to themselves. Sims had been looking out of the window, but only then seemed to realize where they were. He looked round quickly at Frank and Les, and cleared his throat nervously: 'Look here,' he said, 'I think I owe you both an explanation.'

Les grinned. 'Nah, sir, no need for that. We understand.'

'I don't think you do, Gill. The fact of the matter is, I must ask you both to give me your solemn word that you will tell no one of the . . . the circumstances in which we met this afternoon.'

'Good as a wink, eh, sir? Trust us. Ain't that right, Frank?'

Frank grinned and nodded.

'Besides,' Les said, pointing at the basket, 'it's like striking a blow, ain't it? That's what Bert Crocker used to say. He said it was a form of sabotage.'

'Sabotage?'

'Yes. Mind you, Bert Crocker was a bit of a twister.'

'Look here,' said Sims, 'you'd better come and have tea with me at my digs. And I'll try to explain.'

Myrtle Lodge was a large, gabled house set back from the road about half a mile outside the village. It was the home of the Misses Elliott, whose father had been the local solicitor and who had built the house at the turn of the century. Miss Florence was busy trimming the clematis over the porch as Peter Sims, Frank, and Les came up the drive; and sitting on the ground beside her was a small terrier dog. When he heard the gate, the dog jumped up and ran towards them, barking and scampering this way and that.

Miss Florence stepped down from her stool. She was a tall, birdlike woman. 'Ilkley,' she called, 'desist! There you are, Mr Sims. Did you enjoy your trip to the sea?'

'Thank you, yes,' he replied. And explained that he'd met two of his pupils on the way home and had asked them to take tea with him, and hoped that it wouldn't be too much trouble.

'Oh, Mr Sims, how delightful! Agnes is presently preparing our own tray and it will be no trouble at all to make a sandwich or two more. Take them up, do.'

Sims's sitting room was upstairs at the back of the house. '*Dulce domum*,' he remarked, as he opened the door and ushered them inside. 'Sit down, sit down.'

The room had a small, tiled fireplace with well-worn leather armchairs on either side; a dining table with a vase of fresh flowers; and a writing desk. Along one wall there were shelves which were filled with books. And above the mantelpiece were a number of framed photographs: young men in academic gowns and long scarves standing together on a river bank; and one of what looked like amateur theatricals or fancy-dress. And in that one, Frank was almost certain, there was a face he recognized. It was that Mr Forbes-Handley, the Schools Inspector—wasn't it?

'Do sit down, Tate.'

'Yes, sir.'

There was a knock at the door and Sims opened it to reveal the other Miss Elliott, Agnes, holding a large wooden tray on which there were cups and a teapot, and a plate of small, precise sandwiches.

'I'd already prepared tea for Florence and myself,' she told them. 'But I daresay you're all jolly hungry after your travels, so we decided that your need was greater than ours.'

'That is most kind, Miss Elliott,' said Sims.

'Not at all.' She placed the tray on the table and smiled at Frank and Les. 'It is so pleasant to see young faces in the room,' she said. 'My brother Mervyn, Captain Elliot—he was killed during the battle of the Somme, you know, in 1916—he used to entertain his friends here when we were children. So very many years ago. Please eat it all up. And don't hesitate to call if there is anything else you need.' She hesitated at the door. 'So pleasant.'

When she had gone, Sims pushed the plate of sandwiches across the table. 'Do tuck in,' he said. 'I haven't much of an appetite myself. Besides, this really is quite difficult for me. You see, I feel a bit of a fool— though I daresay you don't think there's anything very unusual in that. I don't want to sound melodramatic—I mean, I've never thought of myself as the stuff of melodrama—but such are the times in which we live. The fact of the matter is . . . even though I promised you an explanation . . . to be painfully honest with you, I'm not sure I can explain. I'm not sure I have the right to involve you, d'you see?'

Downstairs the doorbell rang and they heard the dog barking excitedly. Sims paused. 'Where was I?' he said.

'Look, sir,' said Frank, 'you don't have to explain. We won't say anything, honest. I mean, it's like Les said—

135

the black market's like striking a blow against them, isn't it? It's like resisting, isn't it?'

'Black market?' said Sims, the teapot half-raised in his hand.

'Yes, sir.'

'Is that what you think I was doing?'

They both nodded.

'Oh, I see.'

There was a tap at the door and Miss Agnes, with Ilkley under her arm, looked in.

'Do forgive me; I'd forgotten the jug of hot water,' she said. 'We do have to stretch the tea so very far these days, don't we? Oh, for a quarter pound of even passable Breakfast Assam! By the way, there is the most dreadful news from Middelbury.'

'Middelbury, Miss Elliott?'

'Police Constable Carr has just called—he often looks in to see that we are safe—it really is quite dreadful. What a world we live in, Mr Sims! The Germans have shot those poor people they took prisoner—the hostages.'

'Shot them!'

'Such wickedness!' she said, placing the jug of hot water on the tray. 'It makes one's blood boil, doesn't it! But there, I am spoiling your tea-party. Forgive me.'

'No, please,' said Sims. 'When did this happen?'

'It appears the men who attacked the German patrol failed to surrender, so they shot the four men they had taken hostage,' she said. 'It is barbaric! Ilkley!'

The terrier had jumped down from under her arm and disappeared under the table where he was sniffing excitedly at Sims's basket. At the sound of his name he sank his teeth into the teacher's raincoat which was rolled up on top of the basket and dragged it away across the carpet.

'Ilkley!'

'It's of no consequence, Miss Elliott,' said Sims, and got up to retrieve his coat. The dog took this as a sign that he wanted to play and retreated under the desk. Meanwhile, the basket, which had been pulled out from under the table, had toppled on its side.

''Struth!' said Les, looking down at it. 'Frank!'

Frank followed his friend's gaze. And gasped. The covering cloth and the onions had slipped to one end of the basket taking a second cloth with them and revealing beneath it a tangle of wires and what appeared to be part of a clock. Quickly, Les righted the basket and pulled the cloth back into place.

Sims had by now managed to get hold of the dog and was carrying him over to Miss Elliott.

'Thank you, Mr Sims,' she said. 'I must apologize for Ilkley's high spirits. You are a naughty creature, Ilkley. Forgive us.' And she hurried out with the dog back under her arm.

Sims draped his mac over the arm of the chair and sat down. 'Is there something wrong?' he asked, seeing the shocked expression on the boys' faces. 'It's the news from Middelbury, isn't it? Your outrage does you credit, Tate—you too, Gill. Miss Elliott is right—they are barbarians. The Geneva Convention clearly means nothing to such people. We must never let ourselves be deceived by their civilized veneer and their so-very-correct good manners. The Nazis are nothing more than street-corner boys; thugs and gangsters, nothing less!'

'Yes, sir.'

'You really must finish those sandwiches; the ladies will be terribly offended if any are left. What's the matter? Aren't you hungry?'

'Yes, sir. No, sir,' they answered.

'Is it discovering that I'm dealing with the black market has upset you? I'm sorry about that. As I say, such are the times in which we live.'

'We've seen in the basket, sir,' said Les.

'The onions? Yes, not the most dangerous form of contraband, are they?'

'We've seen the rest and all,' said Les.

'The rest?'

They nodded. 'When the dog knocked it over. We seen what's in the bottom of the basket.'

'Have you?' Sims began to scoop nervously at his hair. 'Oh, dear! This is very awkward. I was hoping it wouldn't come to this. I hoped your belief that it was simply contraband of some sort would be explanation enough . . . I've not even seen it myself, you see.'

'It's under the onions,' said Les.

'I think you ought to look, sir. Urgent.'

'Do you, Tate? Yes, perhaps you're right.' Sims lifted the basket on to the table and removed the first cloth and some of the onions. He frowned as he looked down at the shape outlined under the second cloth. 'Is it a gun?' he asked. Neither of them answered. Then drawing the cloth to one side he revealed the tangled wires and clock face in the bottom of the basket. 'Good Lord above! What is it?'

'I think . . . I think it might be a bomb, sir,' said Frank.

'A bomb? Dear me! Yes, I'm rather inclined to agree, Tate.'

'What're you s'posed to do with it?'

'Do with it, Gill? I don't know. But . . . This does rather alter things, doesn't it? Look here, I'm going to have to try and explain myself to you properly. I can hardly ask you to keep silent about . . . about all this if I don't, can I?'

'Yes, you can, sir. 'Course, you can,' said Frank indignantly.

'No, Tate. I mean, absolutely silent. As the grave. There is a great deal at stake here.' He sat back in his chair. 'I'd better start at the beginning. Just before the war, you see, I was at university. Cambridge. I read Classics.'

'All about Greece and Rome, sir?' said Frank.

'Yes, Tate. More or less. The point is, in 1939 when war was finally declared, a number of chaps, chaps like myself who were quite frankly unlikely to be asked to fight—you know, poor eyesight and suchlike—well, we decided that should the worst come to the worst and the Nazis actually triumph . . . ' Sims shook his head. 'It seemed such a ridiculous thought at the time. Well, the fact of the matter is, we decided that should the Nazis win, we would all remain in touch; form a network of— "willing civilians" was the way someone described it. "Sleepers" was another description; people lying low, you see—until the call came.'

'To do what, sir?'

'I don't think we really knew. Whatever was required, I suppose.'

'Like the Resistance, sir?'

'Nothing so heroic, Tate. It was all rather vague. And when we came down in the summer of 1940 we all went our separate ways.'

'Was that when you came to Shevington?'

'Yes. When I saw the post advertised it seemed ideal. I'm rather a retiring person, as you may have gathered. I thought this would be the perfect hideaway. Far from the madding crowd sort of thing.'

'Me and Mill thought that too,' said Les.

'Did you, Gill? Do eat those sandwiches, the dear ladies will be terribly distressed if you don't empty the plate. And so it was, the perfect hideaway, until a few days ago when I received a rather rude awakening. The alarm went off, as it were. I'm afraid the call came.'

'They called you, sir?'

'Oh,' said Sims, scooping at his hair, 'I suspect they were quite desperate, you know.'

'Was it that Inspector called you?'

'Tate?'

'Only, he's the one in the photo, isn't he?' said Frank, looking up at the mantelpiece.

'Dear me,' said Sims, 'you don't miss much, do you?'

'And was it him sent you to Seabourne?' asked Les.

'I was given an address there and a password and told to collect something and bring it back to Shevington.'

'To Shevington, sir?'

'Yes. Sort of a messenger boy, really. It was all very anonymous. I've no idea who the people at the house were; and they don't know me.'

'Struth,' said Frank.

'So now you know as much as I do. I've probably told you far more than I should. But I hope now you understand how vital it is that you tell no one what happened in Seabourne and what is in that basket.'

'Cut my throat!' said Frank.

'Me and all,' said Les. 'What happens now, sir?'

'Now? I have to wait. Someone will contact me, I daresay.'

The three of them stared down into the basket.

'It don't look much, do it?' said Les.

'Perhaps that's not all of it,' said Frank.

'Quite. Perhaps the person to whom I pass it on will have the rest,' said Sims. 'I imagine I am simply part of a chain.'

'It'll be going to the Resistance, won't it!' said Frank.

'To pay back the Jerries for what they've done in Middelbury,' said Les.

'No! I know what it's for!' said Frank. Les and Sims looked at him. 'It's for Hitler's birthday! It's bound to be! They're going to blow something up for a birthday present!'

'Struth alive!' said Les.

And for some reason they all laughed. They were still laughing when Miss Florence Elliott opened the door. Frank and Les jumped to their feet trying to get between Miss Elliott and the table while Sims hurriedly covered the basket.

Miss Elliott smiled. 'It really is such a pleasure to hear laughter in the house again. And how reassuring to see that good manners are not entirely forgotten. But do sit down, both of you. Mr Sims?'

Sims had managed to throw the cloth over the basket but the basket was still sitting there in the middle of the table. 'Yes, Miss Elliott?'

'Agnes has told me of Ilkley's disgraceful behaviour and I simply had to come up and apologize again. He does get so excited, I'm afraid. Ah! Have you finished with the basket? I do hope it was useful.' Then her eyes turned to the onions Sims had taken from the basket and which still lay on the table. 'Oh, I say!' she said. 'It seems an age and more since I last saw such splendid onions.'

'I . . . I bought them in Seabourne,' said Sims quickly. 'For you and Miss Agnes.'

'For us, Mr Sims?'

'Yes. Look here, I'll bring them and the basket down later, if I may?'

'Yes, of course. Oh, how kind. What a delicious treat to have in store. But there, I mustn't interrupt your tea-party any longer. I apologize once more on Ilkley's behalf.' And with that, she went out.

'That was a little too close,' said Sims anxiously. 'I must find a hiding place for this.'

'And then what are you going to do?' asked Les.

'Wait, Gill; it is all I can do. Wait for them, him, whoever it may be, to contact me and tell me what to do.'

'You won't have long to wait, will you?' said Frank. 'I mean, there's only a few days now before The Day.'

'Only supposing our surmise proves correct, Tate: that it is a present for the Führer's birthday.'

'But it's got to be, sir!'

'Do you know, Tate—I hope it is with all my heart.'

Frank and Les finished their cups of tea and Mr Sims took them to the front door and out to the gate of Myrtle Lodge.

'Thanks for the tea, sir,' said Frank.

And Les tapped his nose and said, 'Trust us, Mr Sims. Not a word to a soul, know what I mean?'

'Thank you, Gill. Thank you both. I owe you a great deal. It's rather an obvious thing to say, isn't it—but without your help I suspect I wouldn't be here to say it at all. And Tate?'

'Yes, sir?'

'I hope you hear some news about your father soon. You must never give up hope, you know.'

'No, sir. Goodbye, sir,' said Frank. 'I didn't think he was listening when I told him all that,' he went on, as they walked down the drive. 'Who'd have thought it, eh, Les? I mean, the Toff of all people!'

At the bottom of the lane they stood for a moment looking across the fields to where the Downs were catching the last of the afternoon sun.

'You know what this means, don't you, Les?'

'What's that?'

'Know what we've been doing all afternoon?'

'What?'

'We've been working for the Resistance!'

''Struth!' said Les and he laughed. 'I s'pose we have. What with that and finding out about your dad it's been a bit of a day, ennit?'

Chapter 11

'Oh, you've come back, then?' said Mill sarkily, as Les walked in from the yard.

' 'Course I have.'

'Out the way.' She opened the oven door and slid the tray of bread inside. 'Had a lovely time, have you?'

'I saw the sea,' he said; and sat down at the table. 'And they reckon Frank's dad's alive like the bloke down the Green said he was. That's good news, ain't it? What's up, Mill?' he asked when she didn't answer.

'Leslie Gill! I been worried sick all day, haven't I! That's what's the matter! And you just come in here and start going on about the sea and . . . and . . . I've been worried sick, that's what!'

'Mill, there wasn't no need. You didn't ought to have worried.'

'Oh, didn't I?'

'I'm here, ain't I?'

'Worried sick,' she said.

'I'm telling you, Mill, there wasn't no need to worry. No, and I ain't going to worry any more.'

'Do what?'

'And you've got to stop, and all. D'you hear?' he said firmly.

'Les Gill,' she said, looking at him in astonishment, 'what's come over you?'

'It's like Frank says, if them Crockers—'

'You don't mean you told him?'

'Like you said I ought to do. And know what he said? He said thousands of kids run away like we done and

143

nobody's going round trying to catch 'em. Mill, they ain't after us.'

'Les Gill, can you hear yourself? Frank Tate says so, does he? And the police and the Jerries listens to what Frank Tate tells them, do they?'

'Mill, they've got sabotage and black market people to go after, they ain't going to bother about no ten bob note—they ain't.'

Mill looked over her shoulder in alarm. 'You don't have to shout it all round the houses!'

But Les wouldn't be stopped. 'They ain't!' he said. 'I mean, that don't mean we don't have to be careful, everybody's got to be careful of them Nazis. I mean, d'you hear what they done over Middelbury?'

'Yes, Jack Cowdrey come and told Vera,' said Mill. 'Wicked devils! Here, where did you hear about it?'

'Eh? Oh, on the bus,' he said. 'Look, all I'm saying . . . what I'm saying is we don't have to worry like we have been. Not all the time.'

'Why, 'cos Frank Tate says so?'

'No—'cos he's right, that's why. I was in streets full of 'em, wasn't I? And nobody picked on— Here,' he said, 'close your eyes and hold out your hand!'

'Do what?'

'Go on,' he said. 'And now open 'em.'

Mill looked down. 'Where d'you get these?' she said.

'They're for you.'

'They're Jerry fags,' she said peering suspiciously at the packet of cigarettes.

'I know,' he said, and grinned. 'I got 'em off a Jerry soldier.'

'Les Gill, you never!'

'Mildred?'

Mill slipped the cigarettes into her pinny as Vera Thrale came bustling into the kitchen. 'Hello, Leslie,' she said. 'Mildred, I'm looking for the box of apples that was in the cellar. Are you quite sure you put it back in

144

the same place when I asked you to sort through them the other day?'

'Yes, Mrs Thrale,' said Mill. 'I know that 'cos Mr Thrale told me to.'

'Alec? Did he? How odd. Well, it's not there now. Never mind; I'm sure it'll turn up. You know, Mildred, the more I think about it the more I'm convinced those apples are the perfect offering for the feast on Sunday. Do you realize they were laid aside before the Invasion?'

'Yes, Mrs Thrale, I noticed.'

'A potent symbol. Don't you think so, Leslie?'

'No,' said Les bluntly.

'Les!' said Mill reprovingly.

'Why ever not?' said Vera.

'I don't think we ought to be feastin' at all,' he said, 'just 'cos it's Hitler's birthday.'

'I don't know what's come over him, Mrs Thrale,' said Mill. 'You don't want to take no notice.'

'But I do, Mildred,' said Vera, 'and I should naturally value Leslie's opinion. Well, Leslie? Tell me why you think we shouldn't take part in the celebrations?'

''Cos of what he's done to people,' said Les.

'Who, Adolf Hitler?'

'Yes.'

'Quite so. And I agree with you. But we're not celebrating Adolf Hitler. Are we, Mildred?'

'No, Mrs Thrale.'

Les looked from one to the other. 'What're you doin', then?'

'Spring, Leslie! Renewal! The Time of Green Things, that's what we're celebrating. Didn't Mildred tell you? General von Whatsisname and his cohorts can celebrate whatever they wish, it isn't of the slightest consequence. We shall be feasting the Return of the Light, the Coming of Flora, just as country people have celebrated them since time immemorial. By the way, did you have a lovely time at the seaside?'

Les nodded.

'I must say you're looking more chipper than usual. Do keep an eye out for those apples, Mildred,' she said, 'they must be somewhere.'

'What's all that about?' said Les, as Vera went out.

'You heard,' said Mill.

'She's a case, that's what she is.'

'No, she ain't. It's interestin'—all that about the spring and that.'

'Blimey, Mill,' he said, 'she ain't got you at it and all, has she?'

'I just said it was interesting, didn't I. You had your tea?'

'Yes. I mean, no,' he added quickly. 'No, 'course I haven't.'

'Sit down then and I'll see what I can find. Tell me what they said about Frank's dad.'

Colin was in the back garden when Frank got home; he had the Scouts' Union Jack with him and he was raising it and dipping it ceremoniously. He was concentrating so hard that he didn't notice Frank coming round the side of the cottage.

'All right, Colin?'

'Oh! Hello, Frank,' he replied uncomfortably. And Frank could have sworn he was blushing. 'Did you . . . did you find your dad?'

'I need to speak to Nan.'

'She's out,' he said, 'but ma's inside.' And followed him into the kitchen.

Edie was sitting at the table in her outdoor coat. 'Well?' she demanded. 'Where do you think you've been? I've been waiting for you at the bus stop this last half-hour.'

'We . . . we got off down the road and walked up,' said Frank.

'So what did they say? At the factory?'

So he sat down and told her: about the gatekeeper at what used to be Bell's Precision, and the list his dad's name wasn't on, and what the German had said about some of the skilled men like his dad who'd worked there and had stayed to work for the Germans.

'Not Bill!' said Edie. 'My brother Bill would never work for them—he's too pig-headed.'

'But where is he?' said Frank. 'We still don't know where they've taken him.'

'We know he's alive,' said Edie. 'There's plenty with loved ones as never came back who'd be grateful just to know that.'

'And what about this O.T. lot? The organization they told me about?'

'I don't know what that might be.'

'Nan will.'

'Likely she will. We'll have to wait till she comes in.' Edie got up and began to take off her coat. 'You managed to keep out of mischief, then?'

'Who, me?' said Frank. 'Yes, of course.'

'There isn't any "of course" about it, my lad.'

They had finished tea and were clearing away when PC Carr arrived. Colin had taken the flag out to the garden again and came running to the kitchen door shouting, 'Ma, here's the police coming!'

Frank looked up anxiously and went over to the window. PC Carr was coming in through the gate.

'He's got Nan's bike!' he said; and Edie hurried after him into the yard.

'No need for alarm,' said the policeman, leaning Nan's bike against the wash-house wall. 'She come off top end of the lane not far from Cowdrey's. Jack's bringing her along home. Though she en't too pleased with the arrangement.'

They ran down to the gate and there was Nan being pushed up the lane in a wheelchair. Rose was walking beside her.

'Is the bike all right?' Nan called. 'For goodness' sake, Jack Cowdrey, will you get a shift on. Do you think I want folk to be gawping at me like this?'

'We shall get on a lot quicker, Mrs Tate, if you keep still,' came the reply.

'Look at you, mother!' said Edie, running to her. 'I knew it; I knew this would happen one of these days. I knew it.'

'Don't fuss, girl,' Nan replied. But she seemed badly shaken. There was a deep graze on her cheek and a makeshift bandage tied around her ankle.

'I met them on my way home,' said Rose. 'I tried to see to her leg.'

'Not too much harm done,' said the policeman. 'Nothing a few days in bed won't put right.'

'Don't be so damned silly, Dick Carr,' snapped Nan. 'I en't got time to be in bed.'

'You're welcome to borry the chair.' Jack Cowdrey mopped his brow. 'We got no call for it since Dad passed on.'

'I don't need no blessed wheelchair,' said Nan.

'Thank you, Mr Cowdrey,' said Edie. 'We'll let you have it back soon as we're finished with it.'

'I shall put in a report, Mrs Tate,' said PC Carr; and turned to Edie. 'She reckons it was a lorry-load of soldiers put her in the ditch.'

'Blessed hooligans,' said Nan. 'Roaring around the shop like things possessed. They've gone mad this last day or so.'

'I shall pursue the matter, Mrs Tate, never you fret.'

'Much good it'll do. They're a law to themselves, Dick Carr.'

PC Carr and Jack Cowdrey said goodbye and went off down the lane while Frank wheeled Nan to the back door. She tried to get up but seemed very tired, and didn't resist when Edie helped her from the chair and walked her slowly along the hall to the stairs.

'Poor old Nan,' said Colin.

'It's one of them bloomin' days, if you ask me,' said Rose gloomily.

'What's the matter?' asked Frank.

'I ain't been asked, Frank,' she said. 'To help at the banquet. Mr Jarvis the butler told us this afternoon. They don't want us there.'

'I don't know why you thought they would in the first place,' said Colin.

'Oh, go and play with your stupid flag!' said Rose.

'It's not stupid. It's you who's stupid. It's going to be the very highest-ranking generals and people like that at that banquet. They wouldn't want you looking after them.' And Colin turned and walked out into the garden.

'Oh, Frank. I wasn't half looking forward to it,' said Rose.

But Frank was watching Colin through the window. The very highest-ranking generals? That's what he'd said, wasn't it? Yes—he had. The very highest. And they were. And he was right. Dead right. All of them. All the Jerry big-wigs and their Nasty pals! All in one place, all at the same time!

'Joycie Prout was sure they'd want us to serve at table,' said Rose. 'But they're using German soldiers instead. It's not fair. I've been looking forward to it, Frank, I really have. It'd be so lovely.'

He nodded. 'Yes.'

'I knew you'd understand,' she said; 'nobody else does. Ma nor Nan. Oh, Frank, I really wanted to be there.'

'But not that night!' he said suddenly.

'What?'

'You mustn't be there that night, Rose,' he said, and put his hand on her sleeve. 'You mustn't!' Because it was obvious now. Of course it was! Sitting round the table, all of them together? It was the perfect target. 'Not with all those Nazis, Rose. You can't!'

'Don't say that, Frank. Don't say that—not you as well!'

'But they're murderers, Rose; they killed those people over at Middelbury. They did it in cold blood. Rose?'

149

Rose stood up, wiping her eyes with her hand. 'Frank Tate, you don't . . . ' she said, 'you don't understand either—nobody does.' And she hurried from the room.

'Rose? You don't understand . . . ' Why? Why hadn't it dawned on him before? Until Colin said it like that? It was the Nazis and their generals they were going to blow up. Mr Sims's bomb was on its way to Shevington Hall. And Frank Tate and Les Gill had helped to deliver it!

Edie came downstairs. 'I told Nan as best I could about your father,' she said. 'But she wants you to tell her yourself.'

She was propped up on the pillow and looked tired and small.

'Are you all right, Nan?'

'I've got a pain in my head,' she said. 'But I shall be all right. I've got to be. Now sit down, Frank, and tell me what happened. Tell me about Bill.'

So he sat on the faded counterpane and told her. And when he'd finished she said quietly, 'We never gave up, did we?'

'No, Nan. Consider Garibaldi, eh, Nan?'

'Consider Garibaldi, Frank.'

They looked up to the wall beside her bed where the bearded man in the red shirt, arms folded, gazed unblinkingly into the sun.

'It ain't finished yet, Frank,' she said. 'But I believe we're going to find him.'

'What about Betty Firth? You reckon she'll write to this organization the woman at the Town Hall told me about? You know what she's like, Nan.'

'I've told Edie that since I'm laid up she'll have to go and sort it out with her.'

'Edie?' he said doubtfully.

'No need to look like that. There isn't time to waste. And it en't likely as Betty Firth would listen to you, is it?'

'No, Nan,' he admitted. 'Shall I leave you to sleep now?'

'No,' she said. 'Sit there and tell me about that list again—the one his name weren't on.'

So he did. And wished with all his heart he could tell her all the rest he knew. Tell her that there was going to be some paying-back done: that somebody was fighting back. And that he was helping them to do it.

'Gargery? Are you there? Puss?'

Warden Firth searched the borders and hedge at the bottom of the garden but there was no sign of him. Gargery was a cat of very regular habits and it was most unusual for him not to come in for his breakfast.

She went back inside and sat down again at her desk. She had been there even earlier than usual that morning, but the pile of letters waiting to be typed still seemed to fill the tray. Names, addresses, I.D. numbers, verification of this and confirmation of that, the details the people up at the Hall required were always endless; but these last few days they had been excessive even by Hauptsturmführer Honegger's rigorous standards.

But Betty was determined. Whatever happened, today she would get down to the village: she must. There had been a very decided 'air' about the place last time: something unspoken. She knew what it was, of course, it was this awful business over at Middelbury. It was so unfair. Something like that could undo all the good work she'd put into getting things back to normal. She certainly held no brief for attacks on German soldiers, but shooting those hostages, ordinary Middelbury folk—no, that was inexcusable. And surely the General and his staff realized there would be reactions in the village? She was quite sure she'd seen one or two people who'd been standing outside Dearman's move away when they saw her coming across The Green. And the awful silence when she'd gone into the shop had been too obvious to ignore. When she'd been up in London for the National Conference at the Central Hall, some of the other wardens had told perfectly dreadful tales of the spite and vindictiveness directed against them simply for doing their job—for doing their best.

She looked out across the garden: there was still no sign of Gargery. Where could he have got to?

She must get down to the village and talk to people. But how was she supposed to do that with a mountain of paperwork on her desk? Yes, and a stream of callers pestering her morning, noon, and night? Callers like Edith Worth. If Edith Worth had called once she had called half a dozen times about this business with her brother. The last time, she had stood on that carpet and demanded, bold as brass, that a letter go to the Organization, as she called it, at once. She meant the Organization Todt, of course; the civilian branch of the German army which supervised construction work. She'd obviously no idea how enormous that organization was; or the number of people under its control throughout Europe, building roads, aerodromes, the Atlantic Defences. No idea at all. It would be like looking for a needle in a haystack. Besides, she'd had to be told that for the next day or so all letters would just have to take their turn. But she had been very insistent: disagreeably so. So unlike Edith; she was normally such an accommodating woman. How relentless people could be when you gave them even an iota of hope.

The sound of someone knocking urgently at the front door brought Warden Firth to her feet and she hurried away to answer it. The despatch rider handed her the envelope, saluted, and roared down the path, leaving a choking cloud of exhaust in his wake. She remained on the step for a moment or two, hoping Gargery might have been attracted by the commotion. She called his name, several times, but he still didn't appear. And with a worried glance over her shoulder, she gave up and went back inside.

The letter from the Hall was signed by Hauptsturm-führer Honegger. Everything always was these days. It began with a detailed explanation of the arrangements for the Führer's Address which would be relayed from Berlin at one o'clock on the afternoon of The Day. An English translation was going to be made available for each man, woman, and child; and the Warden was asked, by return, 'at once', to verify and confirm the number required in Shevington and its immediate area. 'At once' made her wince. Did that mean she would have to put off her expedition to the village? She read on.

'You will take especial notice,' she read, 'that as of 09.00 hours this morning new posters have been put up outside all Post Offices and Police Stations within the Southern Area Command warning the civil population of the penalties for assisting or concealing enemies of the Reich. Wardens are required to ensure that all members of the community for which they are responsible are made aware of this matter. The text of these posters is as follows:

'From today, Tuesday 16th April 1941, all activities within the area of the Southern Area Command which may be regarded as constituting opposition or resistance to the German Forces of Occupation or their Civil Representatives, acts of violence, sabotage, civil disobedience, the compliance in such acts of either an active or passive nature, or the assisting or concealment of those responsible for such acts, will be punishable by death without trial.'

Dear heavens! 'Death without trial'! Why, that was little short of legalized—Betty gasped, as the french windows crashed open and the wind sent the curtains billowing inwards.

'Oh, Gargery!' she exclaimed. 'Gargery, you gave me such a fright.' She scooped him up, and stood peering out at the garden apprehensively. Then she quickly closed the windows and fastened them. She walked back to the desk and sat down with the cat on her lap. 'Oh, puss,' she sighed, 'I thought for an awful moment that

153

someone might have—Oh, Gargery, whatever is the world coming to?'

The days since their visit to Seabourne had been difficult ones for Frank and Les. As new workers for 'the Resistance', members of Sims's 'willing civilians', they wanted desperately to be doing something now that something was really being done. At school, they had immediately let Sims know Frank's conclusion that the target must be the banquet up at the Hall; though Sims hadn't seemed as certain or as excited as they were at the prospect. But most of their time was spent simply watching him, like hawks, for any sign that the word had come.

They found themselves keeping themselves to themselves even more than usual. And succeeded for the most part. Except the morning Wally Carr tried to start a row with Frank. Wally had been chosen by Mr Dearman to carry the Scout Troop's pennant during the ceremonies on The Day. Wally had wanted to carry the Union Jack, but that had been given to Colin; and Wally wasn't losing any opportunity to let everyone know that Old Dearman had got it wrong and that Colin Worth was going to make them all look a right lot of dafties. Frank felt an odd sympathy for his cousin when he heard what Wally was saying, and was tempted to take a poke at the policeman's son. But he didn't. He had more important things to do.

They watched Sims in Assembly, out in the playground, during lessons; they watched him as he arrived in the mornings and as he left in the afternoons, waiting for him to give them a sign. But the teacher said nothing. The days passed, two, three.

'You know what I think, don't you?' said Les—after school they had followed the teacher as far as they dared, almost as far as the turn-off for Myrtle Lodge, and were now trudging back through the wood towards Thrale's—'P'raps he don't want us to help him.'

' 'Course he does,' said Frank. 'Why d'you say that?'

'But he must have been contacted by now.'

'He hasn't,' said Frank emphatically. 'He can't have been, Les. He would have told us.'

'Getting close though, ennit?'

'I know. I don't understand why it's taking them so long.'

'It might have got too dangerous. What with them posters and the Jerries killing people like that.'

'But they wouldn't call it off, Les—they couldn't. They can't miss a chance like this.'

They had come down out of the wood and were crossing the open ground behind the house when they saw the car in Thrale's yard. There were two soldiers standing next to it; and not far away, SS Hauptsturmführer Honegger was talking to Alec Thrale.

' 'Struth, Frank, it's him! It's that white-haired geezer!' exclaimed Les anxiously. 'Where's Mill? They ain't come looking for us, have they? Where's Mill?'

'No, look—it's all right, she's there,' said Frank, pointing to the kitchen doorway where Vera and Mill had appeared. 'I don't think it's her they're after.'

They watched as Alec Thrale and Honegger walked across to the shed. Thrale produced a key, released the padlock, and went inside. Honegger followed him in and the two soldiers took up positions either side of the door.

'There's no call for this,' the keeper said, 'no call at all. I don't know how I'm expected to do my job without a gun.'

'A precaution, Herr Thrale, nothing more. Yours is the only civilian weapon, the only legitimate civilian weapon, in the area. It is a precaution until my generals have all gone home again. Then you shall have it back at once.'

Alec Thrale unlocked the chain, and lifted his shotgun down from the rack. As he did so, the soldiers by the door turned their rifles to cover him, but Honegger waved them aside. 'I trust Herr Thrale implicitly,' he said. And smiled. 'But I must also ask him for his spare cartridges.'

Thrale opened a drawer and took out two boxes of cartridges which he handed to the German together with the shotgun.

'That was my father's gun,' he said. 'You're to take care of it, d'you hear?'

'You have my word,' said Honegger. 'I will return it to you personally.'

Alec Thrale took out his key and gestured towards the door; but his visitor was in no hurry to leave. He stood looking round the keeper's workshop. He seemed particularly fascinated by the traps and cages hanging above their heads. He reached up and placed his hand between the jaws of one of the smaller traps. 'Are these mechanisms effective, Herr Thrale?' he enquired.

'They are,' the keeper replied.

'The simplest traps are often the best.'

The soldiers had gone back to the car, and Frank and Les were standing with Vera and Mill watching silently by the outhouse door. But as Honegger and Alec emerged from the shed Vera said suddenly, 'Well I'm jiggered! I've been looking for those.' She pointed to the shelf above her husband's workbench. 'Alec, those are my apples!'

Alec Thrale looked up at the box. 'No, Vera,' he said, 'those are my apples.'

'Alec! Alec, you know jolly well I promised those apples to Warden Firth for her feast.'

'No, Vera,' he said flatly, 'not those; those are my apples. You know my great preference for a russet.'

Honneger sighed ironically. 'Ah, Frau Thrale! What an Eden we must live in, when something as ordinary as an apple can sow such discord.'

'There's nothing ordinary about these apples,' said Thrale. 'If you think that then you've never tasted one.

156

Here . . . ' He took an apple from the top of the box, unwrapped it, and handed it to the German. 'You won't find flavour or texture to beat that the county round.'

Honegger smiled. 'Thank you, no. I must get on.'

Thrale followed him across the yard, and as he was getting into his car, he said, 'I've your solemn word you'll take care of that gun of mine?'

'Assuredly so,' the German replied.

'And what am I supposed to do meantime if I meet a poacher?'

Honegger laughed. 'Put out more traps, Herr Thrale,' he said. 'You can never have too many traps. Good day. Good day, Frau Thrale.'

'I wish you'd told me about those apples, Alec,' said Vera, as the car drew out of the yard. 'I don't know what I shall tell Betty Firth.'

'Tell her what you like,' Thrale replied testily. 'I don't want those apples touched. By anyone, d'you hear? Not by anyone!' And securing the padlock on the outhouse, he turned and strode away towards the woods.

'What's up with him?' said Les.

'Never mind him—what about Vera?' said Mill, watching her hurry back towards the house. 'He's really upset her going on like that about his rotten old apples. I better get in and talk to her.'

'He didn't half go on, didn't he?' said Frank.

'Like a great big kid,' said Les.

'Yes,' said Mill. 'Know what? There's definitely something got into people this last day or two.'

Chapter 12

'Mr Sims? Are you there?' The enquiry, almost a whisper, was accompanied by a light tapping at the door.

'Come in, Miss Elliott,' Sims replied, closing his book. 'Please come in.'

Agnes Elliott appeared around the door, smiling apologetically. 'Oh, Mr Sims,' she said, 'do forgive me. But Florence and I are in urgent need of your advice.'

'My advice?'

'I'm sure you understand these matters far better than we do. And I know I speak for us both when I confess that we've never been entirely certain what that woman's powers actually were.'

'That woman, Miss Elliott?'

'Elizabeth Firth, Mr Sims.'

'The Warden?'

'Quite so. The question is: do you think Florence and I are obliged to attend this rehearsal she has announced? Clearly, we will be expected like everyone else to turn up to the ceremonies tomorrow, no matter how disagreeable the prospect—I must speak my mind, Mr Sims—but do you think we have to go down to The Green this morning?'

'I hardly think so, Miss Elliott. I shall be going, of course; but that's because we have to arrange where the children are going to stand and all that sort of thing. I'm sure you won't be expected to attend.'

'Oh, Mr Sims, that is such a relief! She called on us,

d'you see, the other afternoon, and was so very insistent. Quite bumptious. So like that father of hers. He was a dreadful boor. But there, I mustn't intrude. I'll leave you to your book.' Miss Elliott turned to go, but then turned back again. 'Dear me!' she exclaimed, 'I almost forgot in all the excitement.' She drew a crumpled envelope from the pocket of her cardigan. 'This came for you. It must have been delivered rather early. I'm afraid Ilkley got to it before we came down; I hope you won't be too cross with him.' She handed Sims the envelope, and with a final, 'Thank you again, for setting our minds at rest,' she slipped out and closed the door behind her.

The envelope had his name scrawled across it but no stamp or address. He opened it carefully and unfolded the sheet of paper inside. The dog's teeth had chewed through the top and bottom edge but it was still legible. All too legible. He read it slowly and then sat down in one of the old leather armchairs beside the fireplace. It was obviously meant to arrive days ago. Why had it taken so long to reach him? Why? Why had it come at all? Why had they allowed him time to convince himself that it was over, that the whole thing had been abandoned, that nothing more would be demanded of him? And then to do this. He looked up at the photographs over his mantelpiece: 'Tommy' Forbes-Handley and the rest, with their smiling, brave faces looking back at him. He turned away. He remained sitting there in the armchair for almost half an hour. Then he got up, went over to the grate, and dropped the envelope and its contents into the fire.

Frank and Les were waiting at the bottom of the lane, and saw him come hurrying away from Myrtle Lodge. They waited until he drew level with their hiding-place, and then stepped forward and barred his way.

Sims stood looking at them, blinking uncertainly. 'Hello,' he said. 'What are you doing here?'

'We've been worried, sir,' said Frank.

'Worried?'

'Worried what was going on.'

''Cos you hadn't said nothing,' said Les.

'We wanted to know if they'd . . . you know. We thought you were going to tell us when they contacted you.'

'Oh, I see.' Sims scooped at his hair nervously. 'Well . . . the point is . . . you see, there is actually nothing to tell.'

'Haven't they contacted you?'

'No, Tate; no, they haven't.'

'They must have!' said Les.

'They've got to!' said Frank. 'When will they ever get a chance like this again?'

'I'm afraid I don't know anything about that,' said Sims. 'I'm sorry to disappoint you.'

'But there's still all today to go,' said Frank. 'And tomorrow, if it comes to that. They could still be in touch.'

'I hardly think so, Tate. That would be much too late. I think we should resign ourselves to the fact that they seem to have abandoned the operation.'

'But they can't do that,' said Les.

'I'm afraid they can, Gill.' Sims took out his watch. 'Look here, hadn't you two better hurry along?' he said. 'You're going to be late for the rehearsal.'

And with that he walked away towards the village.

'What is the reason for the delay, Mr Dearman?' the Warden called. 'Your Scouts are supposed to move forward the moment the broadcast is over.'

'I'm perfectly aware of that, Warden,' Mr Dearman replied.

'Then why haven't they done so? I have given the signal. Please be so good as to troop your flag.'

'I'd be happy to,' said the shopkeeper irritably, 'but I can't do so if I haven't got a flag to troop.'

'What do you mean?'

'Colin Worth has the flag and Colin Worth has failed to appear.'

'What? Good heavens, why wasn't I told this earlier?'

'He's normally a very reliable boy; which is why I trusted him with the flag in the first place. We have the troop pennant, we could use that.'

'It won't do, Mr Dearman; it won't do at all! This whole thing is supposed to go like clockwork. We'll simply have to take the flag ceremony as read.'

The choir watched her come hurrying back across The Green. They had been arranged in three ranks under the poles. The school piano had been brought out from the hall and stood facing them on duckboards with Miss Meacher beside it.

'We will take the flag ceremony as read, Miss Meacher,' said the Warden. '"The Song for The Day" follows immediately. I will give you the signal, so . . . ' she raised her arm and then dropped it. 'Shall we try that?'

Audrey Meacher sat down at the piano. She turned to the sullen faces opposite, and she was just beginning to count them in when Colin arrived, the flag over his shoulder and very red in the face.

'I'm sorry,' he said breathlessly. 'I had to help ma. I'm ever so sorry.'

'No excuses!' exploded the Warden. 'None whatsoever! You know jolly well how important this rehearsal is.'

'But, Miss Firth . . . '

'Not one word more! Assume your place.'

Shamefacedly, Colin took his place with the other Scouts.

Miss Meacher counted the choir in once more and struck the opening chord. But the Warden threw up her hands. 'No, no!' she called. 'Thank you, Miss Meacher; but now that the flag has arrived I think we should rehearse it after all. But remain in readiness for my signal. Mr Dearman, the flag, if you please. We will

161

assume that the broadcast has finished and . . . ' Mr Dearman shouted a command and the six Scouts began to move forward. 'Wait, wait!' Betty called. The Scouts seemed uncertain whose order to obey and came to a stop in a ragged line. 'You will have to wait for the applause which will follow the broadcast,' Betty told them. 'Please do it again with that in mind. Thank you, Mr Dearman. And . . . '

They dressed off into line and once again began to march forward. At a command, the rank broke into two halves, which then marched left and right led at one end by Colin's Union Jack and at the other by Wally Carr and the troop pennant. Each half then began to follow a semicircle which would bring the flag-bearers face to face in front of the choir. However, as they were approaching the centre, Colin seemed to lose count of the paces; he looked down desperately at his feet, collided with Wally Carr, and they both went sprawling.

George Poole and Nat Gingell laughed. 'You want to keep clear of him, Wal,' George called. 'He's a danger to man and beast.'

'What's the matter with your Colin,' asked Les. 'That ain't like him.'

'I don't know,' said Frank. 'It's not as though he hasn't been practising. He never lets that flag out of his sight. He sleeps with it next to his bed.'

'It is quite a complicated manoeuvre,' Mr Dearman explained to Betty Firth, as he helped his flagbearers to their feet. But she simply glared at him. And turning towards Miss Meacher, she raised her arm. 'Miss Meacher?' she called. 'Miss Meacher, are you ready for my signal?'

But Audrey Meacher, like her choir and everyone else on The Green, was watching the elegant silver car with its pennants and outrider, which had appeared the other side of the checkpoint. As it approached, the guards ran forward quickly and raised the barrier; then stood to attention beside it and saluted. Seated in the back of the car were two men in uniform, who touched their caps casually in reply. The generals had begun to arrive.

Frank looked at Les, and they both looked across at Peter Sims; but he was polishing his spectacles abstractedly as the car gathered speed and drove away in the direction of the Hall. He didn't seem at all interested.

Warden Firth clapped her hands for attention. Nothing was going anything like clockwork and she was beginning to think there was a conspiracy at work to thwart everything her careful planning was designed to achieve. And when, after several false starts, 'The Song for The Day' finally plodded to a halt, she could no longer restrain herself.

'I must say I found that a very uninspired rendering, Miss Meacher,' she observed curtly. 'Flat and quite without the necessary vigour.'

'Perhaps it is something to do with the nature of the occasion,' Audrey Meacher replied.

'I think you had best explain yourself,' said Betty in astonishment.

'But it's obvious, isn't it?' said the teacher politely. 'Their voices will need to adjust to the new acoustic.'

'The new acoustic? What do you mean?'

'The open air, Miss Firth—what else?'

Betty glared at her. 'Then see that they do so. Adjust, Miss Meacher, if you please.'

'Where do you want this, Warden?'

'What?'

Jack Cowdrey and his brother put down the long trestle table which they had unloaded from their horse and cart. 'It's the table,' said Jack, 'for the food.'

Betty gathered herself. 'Indeed,' she said. 'And chairs? You were going to bring chairs, I recall.'

'They're coming. I can't do everything at once.'

'That is precisely what we are required to do, Mr Cowdrey. And I need you to carry the piano back into the hall. And before you do that let me show you exactly where I want the table to stand. Come along.'

The rehearsal appeared to be over.

Sims had gone to talk to Miss Meacher—they were laughing about something—and so Frank went over and spoke to Colin, who was standing on his own looking very cheesed-off.

'What happened, Col?' he asked.

'I got flustered,' his cousin replied. 'I couldn't help being late and everything. It was horrible. It wasn't my fault, Frank—it was Nan.'

'Nan?'

'She's not s'posed to walk far till she's better, you know that. Well, she has. She must have gone out early this morning. Mum found her in bed in her clothes. She'd done her ankle again. She had to sort her out. And it made me late.'

'Is she all right?'

'She's got another bandage round her ankle and says she's feeling tired, that's all.'

'Frank?' Les drew Frank's attention to Sims, who was now taking leave of Miss Meacher and starting off across The Green.

'It's me who isn't all right, Frank,' said Colin. 'What am I going to do?'

'I don't know; I s'pose you'll just have to practise more. You'll be all right.'

Frank and Les followed the teacher all the way back to Myrtle Lodge, and watched him go inside and close the door. Then they climbed the gate into the field opposite and sat down under a tree.

'We just going to wait?' said Les.

'We ain't giving up,' said Frank. 'Somebody's got to come for him today; they've got to. Can you stay out?'

'Not half! I'm glad to be out and that's a fact. I'll tell you what, Frank, Mill's getting as bad as Vera—she is. They've gone barmy, the both of 'em.'

'How d'you mean?'

'They was only singing this morning, wasn't they! Vera was teachin' her some old song that blacksmiths or somebody used to sing. And there she was joining in like a good 'un.'

'He's coming out again!' hissed Frank, and ducked down out of sight.

Peter Sims was coming down the path; he carried a walking stick, and he had a hiker's knapsack slung over his shoulder. He paused for a moment at the gate, then strode away up the lane.

Frank and Les scrambled to their feet and set off after him. After half a mile, the teacher left the lane and they saw him strike across the fields towards Shevington Woods. He stopped once or twice—on one occasion picking a flower, which he stuck in his button-hole—but then walked on as quickly and determinedly as before.

Peter Sims had been surprised how, having made up his mind, having accepted the course he must take, so many of the anxieties, those terrible, overwhelming anxieties, and the guilt which had pursued him—and those faces smiling from the mantelpiece—had seemed simply to fade away. He wondered if this was the way Heroes always felt?

When he reached the gate he stopped, and stood taking stock of the woods on the other side of the road. He turned and looked back to where, in the distance, he could see the tower of Patfield Church: the angle it made with the gate was the line he must maintain. It was quite simple. The instructions had been very clear. And he had committed them precisely to memory. He went through the gate, crossed the road, and scrambled up the bank into the trees on the other side.

There was no path or track and the undergrowth was thick with briars. After a while, he stopped and looked back to verify the line of his progress. He hadn't gone far at all, but the road and fields beyond were already lost to view. He turned and stood for a moment listening to the silence that seemed to fill the wood; the only sound there was was the hiss and creak of the branches high above as they shifted in the wind.

He was about to move on when in the distance, to his right, there was a movement. He turned his head quickly to look: there, in that sunlit gap between the trees. But the sunlit gap was empty. He frowned. And licked his lips. He was sure there had been something there. It had moved. Not quickly, but with a gliding, graceful motion, slipping from sight the moment he turned to look. Something had been there. His fingers closed tightly round the handle of his walking stick. For all its apparent stillness the wood seemed full of movement now. Everywhere he looked, between the trunks crowding on every side, among the trailing branches and undergrowth. There in that clearing up ahead, he had the same sensation: that something had been there the moment before, watching, waiting for him.

His mouth was dry now. What a fool he had been to think it would be easy. Like a hero? Fool. The fear had been waiting for him here in the wood. Circling him, closing in, closer and closer. And all he seemed able to do was to stand and watch it coming, paralysed, like a climber clinging to a rockface, as the panic overwhelmed him. Where the strength came from when it came he never knew. But, 'No!' he said between clenched teeth. 'Not now! You mustn't! You shan't! You shan't stop me now.' And he stumbled forward through the briars.

Whoever sent the instructions must have known the woods well, because he recognized the tree the moment he reached the clearing: an ancient beech with two huge trunks. He went to it and found the hollow place, just as he'd been told he would. He opened his knapsack and took out the oilcloth in which he had wrapped the clock face and wires. He reached up quickly and placed it inside the tree.

Frank and Les watched him shoulder his knapsack and start back across the clearing the way he had come. Then they crawled from their hiding-place.

'He didn't tell us, Les.'

Les shook his head. 'He don't trust us, that's what it is,' he said. ''Struth, Frank—and after all we done for him and all!'

'I wonder when they got the message to him?'

They had almost reached the road before either of them spoke again. Then Les stopped and said, 'But it don't matter; we still helped. We're still part of it, ain't we? I mean, we was there, looking after him, even if he didn't know it. That's what matters, doesn't it!'

'I know but—'

'And what's more, now we know. They're really going to do it. They haven't given up.'

'Les!' Frank pulled Les down into the undergrowth. The car was parked beside the gate on the other side of the road. SS Hauptsturmführer Honegger was leaning against the bonnet talking to Peter Sims.

'But why, Herr Sims?' they heard him say.

'Why was I walking in the woods?' the teacher scooped his fingers through his hair. 'I've told you, I was simply walking—the way one does.'

'With your bag.'

'What? Yes—with my bag.'

'Why?'

'He's for it now,' whispered Frank.

'No he ain't.' Les snatched a piece of fungus from one of the fallen tree trunks which lay beside them. 'Follow me!' he whispered. And then, to Frank's amazement, he stood up, walked out of the trees, and started down the bank.

Sims and Honegger turned and looked up.

'I found one, sir,' Les called. 'It's a big 'un and all. And Frank's just coming.'

When he heard this, Frank stepped from the trees and scrambled down the bank behind him.

'Sorry we took so long, sir,' said Les.

'It . . . it doesn't matter, Gill,' the teacher replied uncertainly.

'What d'you think of this 'un, then?' Les asked, holding up the fungus triumphantly. 'That's a mushroom and a half, ain't it!'

'It's . . . it's extraordinary,' said Sims.

'You have been looking for mushrooms?' said Honegger.

'Yes,' said Les, 'with Mr Sims.'

'That's . . . that's right,' said Sims.

'I have done so when I was a boy,' said Honegger. 'You do so often?'

'No,' said Sims, 'no, not often.'

'So.' Honegger took the fungus and turned it over. He smiled. 'You are not a countryman, I think, Herr Sims. This could quite easily have been the death of you if you had eaten it. It is most poisonous,' he said and tossed it into the hedge. 'You must take more care, schoolmaster. The woods are a very dangerous place. I advise you to keep away from them in future. Good day.'

They watched in silence as the Hauptsturmführer got back into the car and was driven away.

It was a moment or two before anyone spoke. Then:

'You've been following me, haven't you?' said Sims.

''Course we have,' said Les. 'And just as well and all.'

'What do you mean?'

'Because you never told us you'd been told what to do,' said Frank angrily.

'Ah, I see.'

'You said you would but you didn't. Because you don't trust us.'

'Not trust you? I'm sorry,' said Sims, 'I'm truly sorry if that is what you felt. But that wasn't the reason I didn't tell you what was happening.'

'Come off it, sir.'

'I can understand your sense of betrayal, Gill. And I'm sorry. However, I assure you my motive for not keeping you both informed was not the one you ascribe to me. As I tried to explain to you the other day, I gave my word to my friends that when the time

168

came I would do whatever was required. After a great deal of soul-searching, I decided that since it was my word which was given, and the time had come, it was my duty and mine alone to keep that word. Let me finish, please. I decided that I had no right to place anyone in danger other than myself. These people, men like him,' Sims looked along the road, 'that man had those poor fellows in Middelbury killed in cold blood. Honegger and his kind are quite without mercy or decency. The danger they represent is a very real one and I had no right to ask you or anyone else, no matter how willing, to share it. Do you understand what I'm saying? It was no slur on your courage or probity. I owe you both too much for that. Twice over now. Do you understand, Gill?'

'I s'pose so,' said Les.

'Tate?'

Frank nodded.

'I hope you do. I shouldn't care to lose your friendship, you know.'

'But now what happens?' said Les.

'Now it is up to the others. I just hope it's not too late.'

Ted Naylor saw Keeper Thrale before the keeper saw him. He turned and went crashing away through the undergrowth with Thrale in pursuit, slashing at the branches with the stout stick he carried in place of his shotgun. But his quarry was a fly one, and Thrale soon found himself standing alone in a large clearing and the fugitive nowhere to be seen.

The young man watched him from the darkness of the holly bush. A rabbit's head lolled from the neck of the sack he carried over his shoulder; its eyes were filled with blood, and its lips were drawn back to reveal its small, white teeth. He waited a moment or two, listening; and then stepped out into the light.

169

'Afternoon, Mr Thrale,' he said.

'I thought I'd lost you good and proper,' said the keeper. 'I hope you never come poaching my patch in earnest, Ted Naylor.'

'Perish the thought, Mr Thrale.' The young man grinned, creasing the dark bruise on one side of his face. 'Bit of a dance, I know. But it's for the best. We'll not be overlooked here. You've something for me?'

'I have,' said Alec, reaching into his game-bag. 'I've had it with me every afternoon this week. What was the delay? Where have you been?'

'I've been here, don't you fret.'

'Damned if I saw you, then.'

'Weren't no point being seen. Not till today.'

Thrale handed him a small packet about the size of a half pound of butter. 'Don't seem big enough to do any damage,' he said.

'In the right hands, Mr Thrale.'

'And, here,' Alec reached into his bag again and took out what looked like two of his coveted apples, the russets wrapped in newspaper. 'I thought you might want these as well.'

'If they're as tasty as the last 'uns you gave me they'll be a treat and no mistake.'

'That's the lot,' said Thrale. 'That's all that Carey chap gave me: the four hand-grenades and that lump of plasticine or whatever it is. To keep against the day. The other chap, the toff, who called the other morning, the one who said he was the Schools Inspector, he didn't mention anything else. Will there be more?'

'There will, if I have my way. We're only just starting.' Ted placed the grenades and explosive in the bottom of his sack next to Peter Sims's parcel, and settled the dead rabbit on top of them.

'Is it Shevington Hall you're after?'

'What you don't know you can't tell, Mr Thrale. No offence, I hope.'

170

'None taken.' Alec Thrale held out his hand. 'Good luck to you.'

'Yes,' said the young man, taking it, 'we shall need plenty of that.'

Chapter 13

Despite a glass of warm milk before going to bed, and the no-nonsense lecture she had given herself—After all your meticulous preparations, Elizabeth Firth, you know jolly well there is no earthly reason why tomorrow's proceedings shouldn't go anything other than swimmingly!—the Warden slept badly. And was awake well before six. She got up and went downstairs to make herself some breakfast. There was drizzle on the window and grey clouds above the trees at the end of the garden. Still, she reminded herself: Rain before seven leaves off before eleven. There was every prospect that by midday the sun would be shining. She finished her breakfast, fed Gargery, and went back upstairs to wash and dress. She chose her navy two-piece and a plain, cream blouse. Was it a little severe? Perhaps. But it did seem to strike an ideal balance between the serious and the celebratory aspects of the occasion. Did it? She relented; and pinned the marcasite brooch her father had always liked to see her wearing, a knotted ribbon arrangement, to her left lapel. Shoes? It would have to be the brogues. The Green could be treacherous on a day like this. When she'd finished, she hurried back downstairs, collected her macintosh and umbrella from the hall, and went into the office.

'Time to go,' she announced. 'Gargery, I'm going now.' The cat looked up briefly from his cushion.

She checked the contents of her briefcase: the timetable; her copy of 'The Song for The Day'; the translations of the Führer's speech, which had been delivered from the Hall the previous evening; some aspirins; and the notes she'd made—just in case she was asked to say a few words.

She was making a final adjustment to her hat in the hallstand mirror when she heard the motorcycle arriving outside. Oh, no, not today—please! But when she opened the front door there was the familiar courier waiting on the step. He handed her the satchel and ran back to his machine, which then roared away scattering the cinders from her front path in all directions. Betty emptied the satchel on to the hall table. Mercifully there was only a handful of letters: four official-looking, buff-coloured ones, and one of the flimsy, fold-up sort the Red Cross issued. Well, the official ones would just have to wait, she decided. Yes, even the two marked: Urgent. The Red Cross one would be for Edith Worth and she could take that with her. She slipped it into her briefcase, and closing the front door behind her, hoisted her umbrella and stepped out resolutely into the rain.

'He's got a nice day for it,' observed Nan.

Frank took the cup from her and placed it on the table next to her bed. 'You're sure you don't want me to stay home, Nan?' he said. But the offer was half-hearted, and he knew it. The place he wanted to be was down on The Green. Because, when he'd thought about it, and he'd thought of little else, it might not be the banquet! It could happen any time during the day. Any time the generals were all together. All in one place and—Bang! And the village would be the place the news would come first. And he wanted to be there. 'I mean, I will if you want me to.'

'No,' she said, easing herself up on the pillow and drawing the old overcoat round her shoulders. 'You go on. Besides, I want you down there listening.'

'Listening?' he said.

'And watching,' said Nan. 'You'll be my eyes and ears

today. A day like today, Frank, there's no knowing what folk're likely to say and do. Go on, off you go. And come home and tell me every detail.'

'Yes, Nan.'

'You can't stand about all morning on an empty stomach, Colin.'

'I've got the belly-ache, ma. I've been out-the-back twice already.'

'That egg will bind you. There!' Edie drew her sleeve along the brim of Colin's Scouts' hat, which she was turning slowly in the steam from the kettle. 'See that, Rose?' she said. 'See how it brings up the nap? I used to do your father's trilby like this. Colin, sit down and finish that egg!'

'I've got to go again.'

'What am I going to do with him?' she asked, as he hurried out. 'He's in a proper state.'

'I don't know why,' said Rose. 'He's only got to lift an old flag up and down.'

'Oh, try and have a bit of sympathy, girl, do! Frank?' Edie turned as Frank came in from the hallway. 'How does she look?'

'Better,' he said. 'And she drank her tea.'

'That blessed jaunt's taken more out of her than she's letting on. Whatever possessed her to go out like that? Will you be coming down to The Green with us?'

'I said I'd meet Les first.'

'Mind you behave yourselves.'

'Cheerio, Rose,' he said from the doorway. But Rose didn't answer.

Edie began to collect up the breakfast dishes. 'Shake a leg, girl!' she said. 'You can't sit in your dressing-gown all morning.'

'I might as well.'

'I hope you're not still moping about not going up to the Hall. I've told you, you're better off out of it—you

174

and Joycie Prout. Nice girls like you don't want to be bowing and scraping to that lot all night long.'

'Yes, we do,' said Rose.

Edie turned from the sink and looked at her daughter. 'I beg your pardon, Rose Worth?'

'You don't understand. You don't. Nobody does.'

'Oh yes I do. I've told you, you're better off out of it.'

'I know you've told me,' said Rose angrily. 'Everybody has! You, and Frank—he's had a go at me, and Nan—she's had a go at me; you all have. None of you understands.'

'Don't you go on like that to me, my girl!'

'I don't know what you all take me for.'

'And what's that supposed to mean?'

'I'm not daft. I know they've done bad things. I know how cruel and wicked the Jerries have been. I do! I just wanted to see it, that's all. I just wanted to see all the smart uniforms and candles and the beautiful things. That don't mean . . . It don't mean I'm bad.'

'Bad?'

'It don't mean . . . It don't mean I'm glad they won or that I don't want our dad to come back,' the words came tumbling out. 'It don't mean that!'

'Good heavens above, girl,' said Edie, 'whoever said it did? Rose?' Rose looked away. 'Rose? Whoever said such a wicked thing?'

'Nobody,' she said.

'Is that what you've been thinking? Have you been thinking that about yourself? You have, haven't you?'

'Yes,' she said quietly.

'It don't mean anything of the sort! And there's nobody in this house thinks that it does,' said Edie. 'Rose, d'you hear?'

'Oh, ma—I know I went on about it all the time. I know that. Because I was looking forward to it, that's all. It was something to look forward to. Something nice. You've got to have something to look forward to.' She looked up from the table. 'You've got to, ma. Ma?'

175

Her mother looked at her and nodded. 'Yes,' she said quietly, 'you've got to have that.'

'That's all it was.'

'I know. Go on—you go on up and put your bit of tidy on. Go on, girl. I'll sort Colin out and we'll all go down The Green. I can't remember the last time we all went out together, can you?'

Hunched against the rain, which had at last begun to ease a little, Frank and Les made their way down the lane towards the village.

'Think we might be wrong about the banquet, then?' said Les.

'Well, I've been thinking about it,' said Frank, 'and I reckon they'll try and get them whenever they can— whenever they're all in one place. All those Nazis and generals together. So it could be any time today, couldn't it?'

'What, like while they was all sitting there listening to the Boss on the wireless?'

'All together, yes.'

The sound of a horse on the road made them stop; and they turned to see Jack Cowdrey's cart coming towards them. The farmer pulled up next to them. 'You two want a lift down to The Green?' he asked.

'Yes,' they replied. 'Yes, please!'

'Hop on, then.' They clambered up beside him and the cart set off again along the lane. 'This is my last journey,' he told them, indicating the chairs in the back of the cart. 'I've been collecting these all morning. How's your Nan, Frank Tate?'

'Her ankle's still bad. She went out the other morning and walked too far on it.'

'She ain't coming today, then?'

'She's home in bed.'

'She's in the best place.'

They had turned out of the lane on to the road to the village when a sudden blast on a car horn made Jack Cowdrey pull hard on the reins as the horse reared in alarm. Escorted by an open-topped lorry full of soldiers, a car with pennants flying from its bonnet and the insignia of the Wehrmacht posted along its bumper was trying to pass them in the narrow space. When it was obvious it wouldn't be able to, the soldiers jumped down from the lorry and ran forwards.

'You must move aside,' their sergeant called. 'Quickly! Quickly!'

'Open up that gate for us, boys,' said Jack. 'I'll have to back into the field to let them go by.'

Frank and Les got down, opened the gate, and Jack backed the cart off the road. The soldiers had formed a line between the car and the cart, and were standing with their rifles levelled. 'Jumpy, en't they?' said Jack under his breath. 'We're going to have to watch our p's and q's today, all right.'

The silver car slid by and they glimpsed the impressively uniformed figure in the back.

'He'll have landed on the strip t'other side of Patfield,' said Jack. 'That's why they're on this road. Coming and going all yesterday they were.'

'Where from?' asked Les, as the soldiers clattered away and climbed back into their lorry.

'France,' said the farmer. 'Yesterday it was food; filled a damn great lorry with it. Sausage and champagne up the Hall tonight, you can be sure of that. Giddup!'

In the middle of The Green the wooden poles had been strung with bunting, Union Jacks, and swastika flags. A portrait of Hitler was suspended from the crosspiece, and below it hung a loudspeaker. On a table next to the poles stood a large wireless set. A soldier sat beside the table and another was standing behind it. From the speaker above came the sound of a military band.

'When did they do all this?' said Frank.

'She's been down here since first thing this morning. It's been non-stop,' said Jack.

Not far from the school gates, a trestle table had been set up with a tea-urn at one end, and, under Warden Firth's supervision, was being spread with dishes and jars. The school piano, covered in a sheet of tarpaulin, was already in its place close to where the choir would stand.

Frank and Les helped Jack Cowdrey unload the chairs, and were walking across to join Peter Sims when Margie Prout stopped them.

'Here, you two,' she said. And pulled two sheets of paper from the bundle she was carrying.

'What is it?' asked Frank.

'It's what Hitler's going to say,' she said. 'You won't know what he's talking about otherwise, will you?'

'I don't want to know what he's talking about.'

'Oh!' she said. 'Don't be so awkward, Frank Tate! You've got to have one. Miss Firth says so.'

She pressed the sheets into their hands and went off in pursuit of George Poole and Wally Carr, who were standing by the table admiring the wireless set.

'Good morning, Tate. Good morning, Gill,' said Sims, who had obviously received a visit from Margie earlier.

'Morning, sir. Have you read it?'

'What's it say?' asked Les.

'Not much in what you could call the birthday mode, Gill,' he replied. 'But then, I have difficulty envisaging the Führer tucking into jelly and sticky buns, don't you? Or playing Pass the Parcel with his chums? It's mercifully, and unexpectedly, brief. Mostly about Russia. He does seem terribly confident about his invasion of Russia.'

'It was on the films the other night,' said Les.

'Reckoned nothing could stop him,' said Frank.

'Yes,' said Sims. 'As I recall, Napoleon Bonaparte entertained a similar delusion. *Cave*, you two, isn't that the SS type?'

Hauptsturmführer Honegger's car drew up next to the checkpoint and Honegger got out. He spoke briefly to the guards by the sentry-box and then turned to inspect the activity on The Green.

Busy with the chairs and tables Betty Firth didn't see him at first. When at last she did he had turned back to the guards. For a moment she hesitated, watching him. Such a fine looking young man in his dress-uniform, cap, and polished riding-boots. That would be in honour of the generals, of course. So smartly turned out. Could he really be the one who had had those poor people in Middelbury executed? Oh, dear, he had seen her now! And he was beckoning.

'Everything is in order,' she assured him, hurrying across the wet grass. 'All quite according to the timetable. Not many people have arrived yet. It is quite early.'

She had seen it before—dozens of times—but as she stood in front of him Betty found that her eyes were drawn uncontrollably to the small metal skull gleaming on the Hauptsturmführer's cap.

'Warden Firth?'

A murderer? But he didn't look at all like those awful types one saw from time to time staring out of the pages of the newspaper. Men with furtive eyes and crumpled collars standing at the top of steps or being hauled away by a policeman. He wasn't like that. No. Oh, dear! Dear Lord, no—of course he wasn't! *Because he was the policeman!* Her horrified gaze slipped from his cap to his face. A policeman who murdered people! And he would do it again. And again and again. Wasn't that what those awful posters of his had promised? Where would it stop? And how many others would have to die?

'Warden Firth.' The Hauptsturmführer was looking at her. And he was frowning. 'Warden Firth?'

'What? Oh, heavens! Please forgive me,' she replied quickly, rallying herself. 'I was . . . I was thinking, that was all. There is so much to think about. I'm so sorry. So sorry.'

'This visit must be brief. To remind you only of the procedures and limits agreed for these celebrations.'

'Quite so.'

'Should you require assistance . . . '

'Assistance?'

'Should your timetable not go according to plan in any way, in any way at all, the personnel at the checkpoint, and their colleagues,' he looked across to the guards by the wireless table, 'have been given instructions.'

'Oh, no! No,' she said quickly. 'I'm quite sure that will be unnecessary. We are all determined to make it a day to remember.'

'I'm delighted to hear it. I shall look forward to receiving your report this evening.'

'A report?'

'It need not be long.'

'Very well.'

'*Heil Hitler!*'

And with that, Honegger got back into his car and was driven away.

By a quarter-to-one the rain had finally stopped, but the skies remained overcast and threatening. Most of the villagers had assembled on The Green; the choir had been formed up, and Mr Dearman and his Scouts were in their line opposite the flag-covered poles. The Thrales and Mill were among the last to arrive.

''Struth, Les!' Frank whispered. 'See what Alec's got?'

Alec Thrale was carrying the box of his favourite apples. But it wasn't the keeper who was causing the heads to turn.

'Never mind his rotten apples,' said Les, 'look what she's done to Mill!'

Vera and Mill were dressed from head to foot in bright green. And Mill was carrying a large bunch of daffodils. When they reached the edge of the crowd, Vera took a flower from the bunch and presented it to Agnes Elliott, who was sitting beside her sister with Ilkley on her lap.

'For you, Miss Elliott,' she said. 'As a token of the Turning Year.'

'For me, Mrs Thrale?'

'To welcome Spring and the Return of the Light.'

'What a delightful gesture!' Miss Elliott took the flower. 'Why, you are a breath of spring in yourself, both of you. Is there one for Florence?'

'There is one for everyone.'

Vera and Mill were immediately surrounded by all the smaller children who were each given a flower and who then pursued them as they passed through the crowd distributing daffodils on every side.

Outrageous! Quite unforgiveable! Betty looked at her watch. If there had been time she would not have allowed Vera's behaviour to pass unremarked. However, as it was . . . She clapped her hands.

'Thank you? Your attention? Thank you?' It took some time for her to achieve silence. 'The Broadcast will commence in a matter of minutes,' she said, 'and I need to know if anyone hasn't received their translation?' There was no reply. 'Splendid. And you all know, of course, that immediately afterwards there will be a short ceremony involving the trooping the flag by our Scouts and the singing of "The Song for The Day". When that is over, I hope you will all remain for the feast to which everyone has contributed so generously.' The music from the loudspeaker died away and Betty held up her hand. 'I think it is about to begin.'

'Ladies and gentlemen, we are taking you now to Berlin,' the announcer told them, 'where our correspondent, William Joyce, is waiting to describe the scene outside the Reichstag in the final moments before the Führer's address.'

There was a silence. The familiar voice—William

Joyce, Lord Haw-Haw, the traitor whose drawling tones had sneered at them from the safety of Berlin throughout the war—began to speak:

'From early this morning, crowds that can be numbered only in their hundreds of thousands have been gathering in the streets of this great city. An hour ago, I went out among them along what must surely be one of the noblest thoroughfares in the civilized world, green with the first signs of blossom, and lined with architectural glories of which Athens in its prime might not have been ashamed, the Unter den Linden. I paused beneath the mighty Brandenburg Gate, rubbing shoulders with visitors and delegations from every corner of the Reich. Units of the Armed Services, members of the Hitler Youth, and Representatives of the National Socialist Party from every country in the New Europe. And everywhere, on every side, the people of Germany: men, women, and children—fathers with youngsters on their shoulders and mothers with babies in their arms; young men and women strolling hand in hand; the old, who have lived to see the world transformed. And on every lip the name of one man: Adolf Hitler. The warmth—it is no exaggeration to say, the love—with which he is regarded is immensely moving to observe.

'I look down now, and filling the area in front of the balcony from which he is to speak and out into the streets beyond there stretches an endless sea of swaying colour, of flags and standards, fluttering in the spring sunshine. Across the city, from steeple and tower, the hour is sounding. I'm looking across to the balcony area and . . . yes . . . there is a movement now and the long windows at the rear have been opened. I can see the figure of Field Marshall Göring . . . and now Doctor Goebbels . . . they have come forward . . . they are waving and smiling . . . and there . . . there . . . ' The words were drowned by the roar of the crowd. And the Führer began to speak:

'*Ich bin überzeugt, daß das Jahr 1941 das entscheidende Jahr für die Neue Ordnung in Europa sein wird. Der Kreig ist zu seiner primitiven Form zurückgekehrt. Der Kreig von Menschen gegen Menschen weicht einem anderen Kreig—nämlich dem Kreig um den Besitz großer Lebensräume. Heutzutage ist Kreig nichts anderes als ein Kampf um die Reichtümer in der Natur. Aufgrund eines eigenen Gesetzes gehören diese Reichtümer demjenigen, der sie erobert.*'

How they roared. Frank could see them; the way he'd seen them so often on the newsreels. Always the same. The excited faces, rank after rank, eager and smiling, straining forwards, trying to get closer, even their salute looked as if they were trying to reach out to him, to touch him. And there on the balcony, or on a platform at the end of some great hall or arena, or gliding past in his open-topped car, the familiar, grim figure. He wondered if all those generals up at the Hall would be leaning forward like that? And that Honegger, too? All waiting for him to tell them what to do?

'*Wichtig ist, daß der Bolschewismus ausgerottet werden muß,*' the loudspeaker barked. And cheers rang out.

'*Die Weltgeschichte kennt drei Vernichtungsschlachten: Cannae, Sedan, und Tannenberg. Wir können unsere Schlachten in Polen und im Westen dazuzählen und die, die wir im Osten kämpfen.*' Again the cheers rang out.

'*Was hier jetzt passiert, wurde von vielen als unausführbar angesehen. Ich habe meine ganze Macht einsetzen müssen, um es zu erzwingen. Nebenbei möchte ich bemerken, daß ein großer Teil unserer Erfolge von Fehlern herrühren, die wir den Mut hatten zu machen.*

'*2,500,000 Gefangene . . . 22,000 zerstörte oder eroberte Geschütze . . . 18,000 zerstörte oder eroberte Panzer . . . mehr als 14,500 zerstörte Flugzeuge . . .*'

What was he saying? On The Green one or two people were looking down at their translations, but most were staring in front of them, carefully avoiding their neighbours' eyes. They were all there. Betty Firth had excelled herself. Even the headmaster and his wife were there. And Mr Underwood was wearing . . . 'Les?' Frank nudged Les. 'Have you seen Mr Underwood?' Standing in the front row of the villagers, George Underwood was wearing a medal and ribbon pinned to his jacket.

Waiting at the piano, Audrey Meacher saw Frank Tate grin. She wondered if he had seen it too: the effect the daffodils had achieved. What a clever person Vera Thrale was. It was such a beautiful idea and so very simple. People were holding them just like candles; candles with bright, yellow flames burning at the end of their green stems. The smaller children, sitting all together, were a positive blaze of golden light. They seemed to illuminate the whole dark and nasty day.

'*Der Kampf um die Hegemonie der Welt wird zugunsten Europas entschieden werden—und zwar durch seinen Besitz von russischem Lebensraum. So wird Europa eine uneinnehmbare Festung sein, die sicher vor jeglicher Blockadebedrohung ist. Im Augenblick ist Eroberung das wichtigste Ziel. Danach is alles ganz einfach eine Frage der Organisation.*'

The long rattle of words rose in a hoarse crescendo and then snapped into silence to be followed by a roar from the crowd which shook the loudspeaker. Again and again. Until, at last, they heard him scream: '*Sieg!*'

'*Heil!*' came the reply.

Three times.

And then there was just cheering. Endless cheering.

Was it over? On The Green people looked at each other uncertainly. Betty Firth waved frantically to Mr Dearman. Colin saw the signal and his sweating fingers tightened around the staff of the flag.

'I shan't be able to watch,' whispered Edie and clutched Rose's arm.

'Shevington Scout Troop,' the Scoutmaster called, 'quick march!'

The line of Scouts advanced with Colin at one end and Wally Carr at the other. After ten paces, the line divided neatly, three turning to the right and three to the left. Each file then made a semi-circle which brought Wally and Colin face to face in the centre opposite the portrait of Hitler. The line came to a halt and turned to the front. Wally and Colin then stepped forward and the troop pennant and the Union Jack were dipped. As the flags came up again, Wally Carr stepped back into line. But Colin remained standing where he was.

'Oh my lord, Rose,' said Edie. 'What's he doing?'

As they watched, Colin Worth solemnly lowered the Union Jack; and then, holding it in front of him, he began slowly to sweep it backwards and forwards, twisting it and turning it into a huge figure of eight. Faster and faster he turned it, until suddenly, bringing the flag upright again, he drew back his arm and tossed it high into the air above his head. Up and up it went, and hung there improbably, as though it was held there by the astonished gaze of everyone on The Green. And then it fell, abruptly and fast and straight into Colin's outstretched hand. There was a gasp, followed by a cheer, and everyone began to clap.

'Hold your dressing!' Mr Dearman called, but it wasn't any good; the Shevington Troop broke up and crowded round Colin. Not that Percy Dearman minded particularly; if the truth were known, he had found the idea of dipping the flag to Adolf rather offensive. Jolly offensive, actually.

'I say, ma!' said Rose.

'Oh, Rose,' said Edie, biting her lip. 'Did you see him? Wasn't he a treat!'

Betty was trying desperately to catch Audrey Meacher's eye. It took some time. When she did, Miss Meacher smiled cheerfully, turned to the choir, tapped the top of the piano, and counted them in.

'Beneath the banner that flies before us,' they sang, 'Under skies of blazing light,

We will raise our voice in chorus
As we hurry to the fight . . . '

When the ceremonies were over and everyone was
sitting at the table or queuing cheerfully at the tea-urn,
Audrey Meacher was delighted by the number of people
who remarked how well the children had sung. They
had; they had never sung better. And what was
especially gratifying was that so many people, when
she asked them, couldn't actually remember what the
wretched song had been about. Only those faces; those
smiling faces with their heads thrown back, still
watching the spot in the air high above them where
the flag had hung suspended for those wonderful,
breathless seconds. Well done, Colin Worth! Well done,
everybody!

'Les thought they might have tried during the
broadcast, didn't you?' said Frank, as they watched the
soldiers unplugging the wireless set and loading it on to
their lorry.

'I think yours is still the more likely hypothesis, Tate,'
said Sims. 'The banquet itself.' He looked across to the
men at the checkpoint. 'Mind you, they've had lorries
full of troops patrolling the area round the Hall all
morning. I passed one as I was coming here. Whatever
the target, it's going to require extraordinary daring; yes,
and a good deal of luck. Well done, Worth,' he said
quickly, as Colin came across to join them. 'I haven't
congratulated you yet on your splendid flag work.'

'Thank you, sir. Did you like it, Frank?'

Frank grinned. 'Pie-hot, Col.'

'Do you know what it reminded me of?' said Sims.
'The *palio*, in Siena. I saw it once when I was there on
holiday.'

'That's the one, sir, the one in Italy!'

'But what is it?' asked Frank.

'The *palio*?' said Sims. 'It's a horse-race. Around the

town square. The tradition goes back to Renaissance times. It's fiercely contested and all the teams have their own special elaborate banners. Before the race they parade them and twirl them just like young Worth here did.'

'It was in my encyclopaedia,' said Colin proudly. 'That's where I got the idea.'

'Well, I can tell you, you did it terribly well.'

'Could I just have your attention? Thank you?' Jack Cowdrey was tapping the table. 'Thank you. If we could have a bit of quiet. And somebody round those little 'uns up. The headmaster is just going to say a few words.'

Betty had finally allowed herself the luxury of a cup of tea and a biscuit and Jack's announcement took her by surprise. This had not been discussed; there had been no prior agreement about speech-making! But before she could intervene, George Underwood was on his feet and had begun to speak.

'I didn't intend to make a speech,' he said, 'but I don't think today can be allowed to pass without something being said.' He paused and looked round at them all. 'Though, as a matter of fact, I believe this day speaks for itself more eloquently than I ever could. It's been a long time since I've seen this Green of ours so full of life, so full of Shevington men and women, Shevington boys and girls. A long time. I rejoice for it. And I hope you do too. Not with any foolish optimism. I think we all know that the road ahead may be as hard, even harder, than the grim one we have travelled these last six months and more. We can none of us know how hard or long that road will be, but when I look around me today it's a road I believe we can travel with hope. And a journey I'm proud to make in your company.'

Peter Sims watched the crowd as the headmaster spoke: he was a dry old stick with his starched collar and watch and chain, but he knew these people and they knew him. And his words seemed to be lifting their heads just the way young Worth's soaring flag had lifted them. They were looking up. Uncertainly, but they were looking up. Like people emerging from a darkened room, blinking in the unaccustomed light, feeling it on their faces but hardly daring to believe it. Oh, what a perfectly splendid irony! Today of all days! The day that nasty little man and his Teutonic bully-boys had hoped to grind their heels in the faces of the conquered peoples of Europe.

'In 1918 I was given this,' said the headmaster, pointing to the ribbon on his jacket. 'It has my name on it, but I have always regarded it as an acknowledgement not of any courage of mine but of the courage of all the men of Shevington who went together into that terrible slaughter and who never came home again. And that is why it has lain in the drawer these twenty-odd years, sharing its place with the dead. Which is why you will never have seen me wearing it before today. But today, this morning, I took it out and pinned it to my chest. I did so because today I want to share it with you; with you, the sons and daughters, grandsons and granddaughters of those brave men I was proud to fight alongside. To let you know, each and every one of you, that I am proud to stand with you just as I was proud to stand with them. And will always be so.'

There was a silence. Broken when, to the Warden's alarm, someone began to sing the National Anthem. The Hall had been very insistent about demonstrations of that sort, of any sort. She looked anxiously towards the dark-uniformed figures at the checkpoint; a phone-call from them would bring a lorry-load of soldiers to The Green in a matter of minutes. But, to her relief, George Underwood held up his hand.

'Let's not give Jerry an excuse for spoiling our celebration,' he said. 'There'll be time enough for singing when The Day does come—our day. And it will. Never doubt it!'

'God bless you, Mr Underwood!' said PC Carr.

'Three cheers for the headmaster,' called Jack Cowdrey. 'Hip-hip!'

When the cheers had died away, and the villagers were crowding back around the table, Betty opened her briefcase to look for the aspirin she'd put there that morning. Which was when she remembered the Red Cross letter which had arrived for Edith Worth.

Edie, Rose, and Joycie Prout were standing together at the back of the queue for tea.

'Oh, ma, can I? Let me go, eh?' said Rose.

' 'Course, Mrs Worth,' said Joycie, 'it's all very hush-hush. Top secret.'

Edie frowned. 'What about the curfew? Follett's farm is miles away.'

'She could come back to our house afterwards. We're nearer.'

'Oh, ma, let me go? I ain't been dancing for ages! Let me go, eh?'

'Careful,' said Joycie softly. 'Here comes trouble.'

'Edith,' said Betty, holding up the envelope, 'do forgive me; I meant to give this to you earlier but as you can imagine I've been—'

'Len!' Edie took the letter from her and tore it open. The single sheet of folded paper which served as envelope and writing surface was small and didn't take long to read.

'What is it? Ma?' asked Rose, seeing her mother's frown. 'Ma, what does he say?'

Edie shook her head. 'Nothing,' she said. 'It's not your dad.'

'Who's wrote you, then?'

'It's not for me, Rose.'

'Go on, Frank,' said Mill, 'it don't taste nothing like it looks.'

'What's made old Thrale part with them?' said Frank, taking the leathery-looking apple she offered him from the basket, and eyeing it suspiciously.

'I dunno. He just brought them over from his shed

this morning. Said Vera could have them after all. She was ever so pleased. I don't know what come over him.'

'I don't know what's come over you,' said Les.

'What's that supposed to mean?'

'To come looking like that. All that . . . all that green and that.'

'Les Gill! Don't be such an old stick-in-the-mud,' she said.

'What d'you call me?' he said indignantly.

'You heard,' she said, and laughed.

'Frank?' Edie held out the letter. 'I'm sorry. I thought it was from Len and I opened it. I'm sorry, Frank.'

'What is it?'

'Look at the front.'

He took it from her. It was his name written there. In thick pencil: Master Frank Tate. And the address underneath it was: Tate's Cottage, Shevington, West Sussex, Southern Area Command.

'Go on, Frank,' she said, 'read it.'

> 'Dear Frank,' it began, 'I am writing this in the hope that you are alive and at your nan's. Because of Hitler's birthday they have let the Red Cross come to the camp and said we can send one letter which is this one I'm writing to you, old son. When they came to Bell's and captured it they wanted me to go on working there but I said no and they arrested me and sent me to ████████ to work on the big road they're building to ██████████. Don't worry about me there are plenty a lot worse off. It is hard work but I mean to come through. And you must too, old son. You must mean it with all your might. I think of you often. Give my love to your nan and remember me to Edie and her children. This is all the paper they will allow us. I must stop now. I think of you often.
>
> God bless you. Love, Dad.'

Frank looked up. 'It's from my dad,' he said.

'Yes,' said Edie, and there were tears in her eyes.

'It is from him, isn't it? It's true. It's from Dad.'

'Yes,' she said. 'Our Bill's alive.'

He stood there looking from face to face: Les and Mill and Rose and Joycie Prout—they were smiling. And suddenly it seemed that everyone was crowding around him. And that they were all speaking at once. And then people began to pat him on the shoulder. And Mr Underwood shook his hand. And so did Peter Sims. And Betty Firth came over and asked what all the commotion was about.

For a long time after Edie and the children had gone Nan lay listening to the empty house. It was rare nowadays for the old place to be so still. So quiet. The heavy tick of the clock in the hall downstairs was the only sound. No clatter of dishes. Or Edie rowing with Rose. Or Edie rowing with anybody. Poor Edie. No Frank and Colin thumping up and down the stairs. The war had filled the cottage with noise. It was a terrible thing to be thankful to a war.

A lorry went by in the lane outside. The Jerries again: the second time that morning. They'd obviously put on extra patrols. It was as though they were expecting something. Nan shifted uneasily on the pillow. But was there going to be anything? And if there wasn't then she was the one to blame. Because there was no way the network could have known that she hadn't been able to deliver the message on time. Should she have sent Frank to let them know? Should she have confided in Frank and asked him to take the message up to Myrtle Lodge for her? No—that wasn't encouraged. John Follett was very insistent on that score. He was right, too. The fewer people involved the fewer who could betray and be betrayed. And never family. Never anyone that close. Nan lay back against the headboard. Well, she'd got it there eventually. She'd done what she could. And to the schoolmaster of all people. He'd always seemed to be such a nervous soul. A rum sort to be involved with John Follett and the rest. Still, he was no more rum, after all, than an old woman on a bicycle . . .

She dozed fitfully. Until, it was not long after one o'clock, she was woken by someone shouting. In the distance. Or was it a dog barking? No—there was no mistaking that voice. She rubbed her eyes. But what was Adolf Hitler doing . . . ? She looked across the room to the open window. It was coming up from The Green. The broadcast must have begun. 'Oh, no you don't, my lad,' she said, struggling out of bed. 'Not in my house!' She buttoned her old overcoat and with the aid of a stick made her way slowly and painfully downstairs. When she reached the kitchen, she leaned against the door-jamb, listening. Just the clock. Either he'd stopped his nasty carry-on or the sound of him couldn't reach the back of the house. She made herself a cup of tea. And after she'd sat and drunk it, she hobbled out into the back garden to see to the hens. She was sure nobody else had.

Which was where Frank found her.

'Nan?' he called, as he came running up the path. 'Nan?'

'What is it, Frank? What have they done?'

'Nan, they've let him write.'

She stared at him. 'What?'

'Look!' He held up the letter. 'It was for me. He's written to me, Nan. Dad. Dad's written me a letter. Look!'

She read it slowly, touching the paper with her fingers. When she finished, she folded the letter carefully and gave it back. 'We can wait properly now, Frank,' she said. 'It'll still be waiting but it'll be different now. Now that we know.'

'Yes, Nan.'

'Give me a hand into the house.'

She put her arm around his shoulder and they walked back along the path together. Outside the back door she stopped and said, 'Does Edie know?'

'Yes,' he said. 'There was a mix-up and she read it first.'

'What did she say?'

'She was crying.'

Nan nodded. 'I'm glad to hear it.'

In the kitchen she sat down in her chair in front of the range. 'D'you remember, Frank?' she said. 'Remember us sitting here that night and what we said?'

'I remember.'

'Remember us saying how we'd go on hoping? And not give up?'

' "Consider Garibaldi", eh, Nan?' he said. And Nan smiled. 'Dad will come back now, Nan, won't he? He will, won't he?'

'I believe he will, Frank,' she said solemnly.

They sat side by side in silence for a while. Then Nan turned to him and said, 'Now then, what about the rest of it? Tell me about the goings-on down at The Green today.'

So he told her about Vera and Mill, and Colin's amazing flag, and Mr Underwood's stirring speech and how the whole village had cheered him.

'I like the sound of all that,' she said. 'And was that the end of it?'

'No,' he replied, 'there's still time.'

She looked at him curiously. 'Still time?'

'I mean it's not over yet, is it? The Day, I mean,' he added hastily.

Chapter 14

The Shevington Arms hadn't been so busy for months; and the extra barrel Harry Poole had wangled from the brewery was going down a treat. Early on, someone had suggested opening up the skittle-alley, and the crash of wooden balls and the shouts and laughter from the back room made it seem like old times. Though there was a noticeable absence of young faces; the younger men seemed to have gone elsewhere for their fun.

Peter Sims had been out walking. He'd walked for miles. He was restless. And angry. He was angry that as the evening turned to night it seemed more and more probable that all his efforts, the trip to Seabourne, his visit to the woods, had been in vain. It surprised him that he felt quite so strongly. What surprised him even more was to hear himself muttering: 'Next time! Next time! I just hope there's a next time!' as he swung at the nettles with his stick.

He had met George Underwood as he was returning to the village; and it was the headmaster who had suggested he might like to join him for a glass of beer. They sat at the headmaster's usual table with the dog, Bess, asleep beneath it. They spoke briefly and in their formal way of the events of The Day. And it was only when they had almost finished their drinks Mr Underwood said, 'Tell me, Mr Sims, do you see yourself remaining in Shevington?'

The enquiry took Sims by surprise. 'In Shevington?'

'Oh, it's not such a bad place, you know,' said the

headmaster. 'Of course, I've not known very many other places so perhaps my judgement isn't the most reliable.'

'No, headmaster,' said Sims quickly, 'I didn't mean that. No, quite the contrary; I've no plans at all for leaving Shevington.'

'Ah.'

'Unless . . . '

'Yes?'

'Has it been suggested that perhaps I should?'

'By whom?'

'I wondered had Mr Forbes-Handley commented adversely on my teaching skills—or rather, my lack of them.'

'Did he mention something of the sort during your interview with him?'

'No. But—'

'He certainly said nothing to me. He spent most of the morning proffering the sort of bureaucratic pomposity and nit-picking one might expect from a Ministry man. Perhaps I should be more charitable. He doubtless has a job to do.'

'I'm sure he has, headmaster.'

'You are very loyal, Mr Sims.'

'Mr Underwood?'

'I believe Mr Forbes-Handley was, like you, a Cambridge man?'

'I believe so.'

'I'm afraid I've more respect for young chaps who put their first-class education to some useful purpose. Chaps like yourself.'

'Thank you, headmaster.'

Mr Underwood drained his glass. 'Well,' he said, 'I must be on my way.'

'So must I,' said Sims. 'It's been a long day. And I rather overdid it this evening. I walked over to Patfield Palace.'

'To the Roman villa? That's a tidy distance. Of course, it's your speciality, isn't it—Rome? Goodnight, everyone.'

Followed by a chorus of 'Goodnights' they stepped out on to the pavement.

'Well, goodnight, sir,' said Sims.

'My son Henry was very fond of those ruins,' said the headmaster.

'I wasn't aware of that.'

'No reason you should be, Mr Sims. He took detailed photographs of the whole site.'

'A priceless record, Mr Underwood.'

'Priceless, Mr Sims. I wonder . . . Look here, would you be interested in looking at them, if I were to bring them in?'

'Oh, very much.'

'Then I'll do so. Goodnight. And I'll see you at school bright and early in the morning.'

'Yes, indeed.'

'Life goes on, Mr Sims. Come along, Bess.'

'Although the weather did prove rather unkind, The Day in Shevington must be considered an unalloyed success.'

Betty wondered about including that remark about the weather. Perhaps it was a little too English? After all, SS Hauptsturmführer Honegger had only to look out of his window to see how grim the day had been. And what about 'unalloyed'? No; no, there was no reason to question that. There was no denying that everything had gone like clockwork. There had been . . . unpredictable elements . . . the decidedly eccentric behaviour of the Thrale woman and that awful cockney creature; and young Worth's peculiar high spirits—what must have come over him? But set against everything else they were really of no consequence and not worth mentioning. As for Mr Underwood . . . the man was living in the past and his contribution had been irrelevant.

'The Führer's address,' she resumed, 'was received with great seriousness and followed by genuine enthusiasm.

There is no question in my mind that The Day will live in all our memories for many years to come.'

Betty sat back in her chair. Her shoulders were stiff and the aspirin had failed to shift her headache. But, it was done now; there really was nothing more to add. She had begun the report the minute she got back from The Green. The news of Nan Tate's son had caused quite a stir, and people had stayed longer than she'd allowed for. Which was all very well, but what with that and then having to supervise the tidying-up she'd got home much later than she'd expected. And that awful young man on the motorcycle would be sure to arrive any moment to take the day's correspondence back to the Hall. She signed the report, folded it, and placed it in its envelope. There were still the four official letters which had arrived that morning, including the two marked Urgent, waiting to be answered.

'No,' she said suddenly, 'no more! In God's four-and-twenty there's only so much a body can do.' She got up, scooped Gargery from his chair and carried him to the window.

She stood looking out at the dark garden. God's four-and-twenty! She smiled. It was what Vi Paine always used to say. Vi, who had been Senior in the typing pool at Merriman and Levy. Whenever it all got too much to bear Vi would adjust those spectacles of hers and say, 'Mr Merriman, if you please! In God's four-and-twenty there's only so much a body can do!' Dear old Vi. And the Farringdon Road, London EC1! How many lunchtimes had she walked its length, scouring the second-hand bookstalls for something to send her father? Her foxed and dusty attempts at reconciliation. She could see it still so vividly: those winter evenings with the lights reflected in the wet pavements and the rain slanting down and driving the umbrellas before it. But they had been . . . Oh, they had been such happy, happy times! And with her own room and facilities to

197

return to each night. Quite her own. Free as a bird. But it was all gone. Last time she'd been in London, for the Wardens Conference, she'd slipped across to Kennington to look at the house where her bed-sitter had been. It had been converted to a leave-hostel for Luftwaffe personnel. And the office, that was gone too. The area around the City had taken a terrible pounding, and the building which had housed Merriman and Levy was a ruin. The basement, where the old postroom had been, was open to the sky, and there were weeds growing along its walls.

'Nothing lasts, puss,' she murmured. 'Isn't it awful.'

There was a knock at the front door. She released the cat, picked up the report, and went out to answer it.

'There is no more?' the courier enquired, as she handed him the envelope.

'No,' she said flatly. 'There is not.'

The courier shrugged, and walked back to his motorcycle.

'And if you don't take more care of my front path, young man,' she called, 'do you hear me? If you don't have a care, I shall make a formal and very serious complaint to your General!'

Alec Thrale knocked the ashes from his pipe against the hearth and stood up.

'Are you going out, Alec?' Vera asked, looking up from her book.

'With the woods full of Jerries? No, I'd like as not get my blessed head blown off.'

'You did warn Leslie and his friend, didn't you?'

'I did. I'm just going to take a turn round the yard. I shan't be long.'

'Sorry, Mr Thrale,' said Mill, who opened the door as Alec was going out. 'Sorry, Mrs Thrale.'

'What is it, Mildred?' said Vera.

'I've brought it back,' she said, holding out the green frock.

'But why? I thought I had explained. It's yours, Mildred. That's why we made the alterations.'

'Mine?'

'I want you to have it. For the next time.'

'Next time?'

'Yes. And we can always dye it again, if you prefer. You did enjoy yourself today, didn't you?'

'Yes,' said Mill, 'I did.'

'Good.'

'I can't say as I thought I would, Mrs Thrale, not first off, to be honest—but I did.'

'I'm so pleased.'

'Thank you for the frock,' she said, and turned to go.

'You're welcome to stay, you know.'

Mill hesitated in the doorway. 'You're reading, aincha?'

'My reading concerns you as much as anyone. All of us, as a matter of fact.'

'What is it?'

'It was my mother's.' The book on Vera's lap looked like a large scrapbook. 'She compiled it when we lived on the farm. Did you know I lived on a farm?'

'I heard, yes,' said Mill.

'I was a city girl like you to begin with, but then we all moved down from Hampstead to a farm over near Datcham. I'm afraid my father and his friends weren't actually very good at it and in the end they had to give it up. It was rather sad. But my mother was an inveterate collector of practical wisdom; she had to be for them to last as long as they did. She wrote it all down. And cut things out of magazines and newspapers. This is my bible.'

'What is it—stories?'

'Recipes and devices; cures, all sorts of old country lore. That's where I learned about dyeing. It's full of things like that. Lessons for survival.'

'How d'you mean?'

'Ways of getting by. Would you like to hear some?'

Mill closed the door and sat down at the table.

They had been watching all evening from the top of the old oak at the back of Thrale's place. Now the wind was rising and the branches swayed beneath them as they peered across the tree tops to where the lights of the Hall twinkled in the distance.

'Anything yet? Anything at all?'

Les, who was a branch or two above Frank, shook his head.

'I thought I saw a car's headlights then,' said Frank. 'You don't reckon some of 'em's started to leave, do you?'

'It's late, I know that.'

'Frank?'

'What?'

'Look . . . I mean, say they don't do it tonight?'

'What do you mean?'

'I just been thinking, that's all. Say they can't? Because . . . I don't know, say that clock and the wires was too late? Say it never got to them?'

'I know.' Frank looked away. 'I've been thinking that. But, Les, we can't just give up, we can't!'

'But it don't mean we have to.'

'What?'

'That's what I've been thinking about. Look, even if that is what's happened—you know, about the bomb and it not being Shevington Hall tonight—just think of all them people: that Inspector, and all old Sims's college pals, and the people at the house in Seabourne, and whoever it was over in Middelbury threw that hand-grenade. Think of 'em, Frank! It's a lot of people. They ain't goin' to give up just because old Hitler's birthday's come and gone. They ain't goin' to give up and we don't have to neither. Know what I reckon? It's just starting. It is—it's just the start. There's people all over the place starting to have a go at the Jerries, giving 'em some of their own medicine. 'Course, there are! It won't happen just like that. Not perhaps just how we'd want it to. And it'll take a fair time, 'course it will. But it's started, Frank, and there ain't goin' to be no stopping it.'

Frank looked up at his friend. 'Blimey, Les,' he said.

'What?'

'Nothing. It's just . . . I've never heard you talk so much.'

'Yes, well . . . ' Les clambered down to where his friend was sitting. 'It's true though, ennit!'

'Yes.'

'Consider Garibaldi, right?'

'Consider Garibaldi.'

'And when old Sims gets the call next time he's going to be coming to us for help, stands to reason. Nah—we ain't going to give up—not ever.'

'Les, what do you think he meant about Napoleon? When he was talking about Russia this morning?'

'Old Sims? Blessed if I know. I can't follow half of what he says. Still, fair dos—he's come up trumps, hasn't he? Turning out to be a good 'un. And trustin' us and that.'

'Careful!' Frank put his finger to his lips. Down in the yard, Alec Thrale had come out of the back door and was standing by the shed. He took out his pipe and they saw the flare of the match light up his face as he struck it and put it to the tobacco.

There was going to be change; as he looked across towards the woods, Alec was convinced of that. They'd be stamping through his covers night after night. 'Nasty' Honegger wouldn't withdraw the patrols now he'd started them. That was the difference, of course: Honegger and his sort made no bones about it—the war went on for all the pieces of paper that were signed and speeches that were made. Honegger's kind were never at peace. They had to go on winning. It was all they knew. All they lived for. Till they'd crushed the life out of you. When you realized that then there wasn't anything else you could do but resist them. Whatever the price.

He looked out across the woods and fields he knew so well. And wondered when the blow would fall.

Shevington Hall was a blaze of light. And from the long windows came the sound of a small orchestra playing the 'Siegfried Idyll', the piece Wagner wrote for his wife's birthday and which Hitler had ordered to be played at all his own birthday celebrations. The music came to an end and there was a buzz of conversation as General von Schreier's guests made their way out of the Grand Salon and across to the Drawing Room, where coffee was being served.

Not long after, SS Hauptsturmführer Honegger appeared at the top of the main steps and signalled for his car. He was followed by General von Schreier himself and General Dieter Brack. The two were old friends and, shaking his hand, von Schreier urged Brack to reconsider and stay a little longer. But Brack explained, regretfully, that it was essential for him to be back in Normandy by morning.

Honegger waited, noting with satisfaction the number of shadowy figures patrolling the vicinity of the Hall and the grounds beyond. An ingenious ant, he concluded wryly, would have found difficulty breaching the cordon he had thrown around Shevington Hall.

General Brack descended the steps, a little unsteadily, and, with a final wave to von Schreier, got into the car. Honegger got in beside him and they were driven away down the dark drive and out through the gates.

Sacks had been hung across the windows and the door, and from outside the barn no light could be seen. Inside, the bales had been pushed back against the walls, and hurricane lamps cast busy shadows as the couples made their way around the makeshift dance floor. A portable gramophone stood on a table at one end, with the records which people had brought with them piled beside it; and guarded by Ned Follett, who was enjoying being up so late. He wasn't enjoying the music much. Especially the one they kept making him play—that Glen Miller's, 'Moonlight Serenade'—the American one that went slow and made them all dance like they were courting. He wondered if that was the reason the Germans didn't allow music like that.

Rose was sitting this one out; sipping a glass of lemonade, and keeping an eye on Phil Gingell, who'd danced with her several times already. He'd told her he thought she looked a bit like Carole Lombard, the film star. Silly beggar—Carole Lombard was much more of a blonde. Joycie was dancing with the sandy-haired chap again: the one from over Middelbury way, Ted Naylor his name was. He was a lovely dancer. The music ended and Joycie came and sat down next to her.

'Give us a sip of your lemonade, Rose,' she said breathlessly. 'Ain't this lovely? It used to be like this down the village hall every week before the war. I'd forgotten the fun we used to have. I seen you dancing with Phil Gingell. Three times.'

Rose smiled. 'He keeps asking me.' They laughed. 'He's a lovely dancer, too—that chap you were with.'

'Who, Ted? I know. It's only luck he's here, and all. He was doing some odd jobs for Mr Follett and Mr Follett told him about tonight. Here, I know what'll get Phil Gingell going—why don't you have a dance with Ted?'

'No,' said Rose, 'I couldn't.'

''Course you could. I'll go and ask him. He's ever so nice.'

'Joycie!'

But Joycie was on her feet and making for the door where Ted Naylor and John Follett were standing. 'Ted?' she said. 'My friend Rose wants to have a dance with you but she's too shy to ask.'

Ted looked over at Rose and grinned. 'She don't look the shy sort to me,' he said.

'Will you, then?'

He shook his head. 'Next time, Joycie. Only I got to be going.'

'You can't go, Ted! It's early yet.'

'I know. But I've got a fair way to travel.'

'Stay and have one more dance. Come on, eh?'

'No, I'd better not. It's getting late.'

'Ted Naylor,' she said indignantly, 'I wouldn't never have took you for an old spoilsport. Well, please yourself!' She walked back to Rose and taking her hand pulled her to her feet. 'Come on, Rose,' she said, 'you and me will have a dance by ourselves.' And she looked daggers at Ted, as Ned Follett carefully lowered the needle on to the record and the music began to play.

'Fit then, Ted?' said John Follett.

Ted Naylor nodded.

'Come on, then. I'll walk you across the yard.'

'Right ho, Mr Follett,' he replied. 'Goodnight, all.'

It was late, but Frank and Colin had not long gone upstairs, and Edie and Nan were still sitting either side of the range. Nan was nodding in her chair, and Edie was darning socks.

'You ought to be in bed, mother,' she said. 'It's been a long day.'

'I'll wait a bit longer, girl,' Nan replied. 'It's been the sort of day you don't want to end, and that's a fact.'

Out in the hall the clock began to strike twelve. 'Must have heard you,' said Edie. And smiled.

'Well, there's a turn-up.'

'What?'

'Don't see you smile like that too often.'

'There isn't usually a lot to smile about, is there?'

'It'll end, girl. Everything does. The Jerries' day will come.'

'We've got to travel with hope, that's what Mr Underwood said. He was very inspiring, mother. He did people the world of good.'

Nan leaned forward and stirred the fire with the poker. 'The waiting is all. That's what your father used to say. But at least we're all waiting together.'

Edie stopped sewing. 'Oh, you should just have seen our Colin, mother,' she said. 'He threw that flag so high I thought it was never coming down again. I did—I thought I should burst with pride. I shan't forget today in a hurry, and that's a fact.'

'And what about the news about our Bill?'

'What about it?'

'Frank said you had a cry when you heard.'

Hurriedly, Edie began sewing again. 'Oh, mother, 'course I did,' she said. 'He's my brother, isn't he!'

They went on sitting, enjoying the last of the fire until: 'Here,' Nan frowned, 'how's young Rose going to get back from Follett's at this hour?'

'She isn't coming back,' said Edie.

'What d'you mean, girl?'

'She's staying over with Joycie Prout till the morning. Oh, mother, I couldn't say no to her.'

'No, 'course you couldn't,' said Nan. 'I'm glad to hear it.'

'I knew there would be. There's a picture of it here,' said Colin, and he brought the encyclopaedia across to Frank's bed. '"The Retreat from Moscow", it's called. That's Napoleon in front. See?'

The column of soldiers stretched away into the distance until it was lost in the swirling snow. The wind snatched at the tattered flags and the rags that were all that remained of what had once been so many proud uniforms. Some were on horseback, slumped in their saddles, while others staggered along beside them, clinging desperately to their stirrups. Men held each other up, hobbling by, bandaged and stained with blood. Some had already fallen and lay grey-faced in the mud beside the road. In one corner, beside the splintered wheels of an abandoned cannon, a hand reached up out of the snow. And on a hill above, a group of fur-clad horsemen sat waiting to strike.

'Why did you want to know about it?'

'It was just something somebody said,' said Frank. 'About Napoleon.'

'It's got everything in it, my encyclopaedia. Like the *palio* in Italy Mr Sims knew about. Anything at all you want to know is here. You can keep it and look at it, if you like, Frank. You can. I don't mind.'

'Thanks.'

Colin went back and got into bed.

'Frank?'

'What?'

'You did think my flag was good, didn't you?'

'I told you, pie-hot, Col. Col?'

'What?'

'What did you do it for?' There was no reply, and Frank turned to look at his cousin. 'Was it to give the Nazis one in the eye?'

''Course. But . . . you won't tell, will you, Frank?' Frank shook his head. 'Mostly it was so ma would have something to tell our dad about. About me. You know, next time she writes to him.'

'He'll be pleased.'

'Think so? Yes, he will. He will, won't he! Can I put the light out now?'

'Yes.'

Frank stayed awake until his cousin's regular breathing told him that he was asleep. Then he reached under his pillow and took out the letter. It was too dark to read it but that didn't matter; he already knew it by heart.

'Dear Frank, I am writing this in the hope that you are alive and at your nan's . . . '

It was shortly after 2 a.m. when General von Schreier was called from the library, where he and his colleagues were enjoying the fine Napoleon brandy which General Brack had brought with him from France but had been unable to stay to enjoy. The brandy and the company of other officers had left von Schreier in a mellow mood.

SS Hauptsturmführer Honegger was waiting in the hall.

'Herr General.' He reported that the journey to the airstrip had been uneventful and that General Brack had taken off safely and would be landing in Normandy according to schedule.

'Good,' replied the General. There was a moment of silence as the two men faced each other. I should invite him back to the library, thought von Schreier. But the absence of the SS man from their celebrations had been a welcome relief. Such a pleasure not to have to measure every damned word and thought. In all truth, the evening had turned out to be the best part of the day.

'Will you join us for a drink, Honegger?'

Honegger smiled politely. 'Thank you, no, General. The Day is not quite over for me yet.'

'Of course. Well . . . Goodnight, then.'

The Hauptsturmführer watched the General start back up the stairs then turned and made his way to his office.

He switched on the light above his desk and picked up the typewritten sheet which had been left there for him. It was Warden Firth's Report. He let his eye run quickly down the page: ' . . . unalloyed success . . . genuine enthusiasm . . . ' He smiled. My dear, stupid, woman—what banal nonsense! They had hated every minute of it. They always did. Hadn't he seen those same closed, angry faces on the streets of Warsaw, and again in Holland when he had been posted there? And it was just the same in France, if Brack's unguarded and slightly tipsy conversation in the car was to be taken seriously. It was always the same. Anger. Hate. Resistance. Well, well, they would learn. And it was his job to teach them. To teach them that they could hate as much as they liked but that resistance was useless.

He looked around the room with its metal cabinets and neat cardboard box-files. How quickly it had filled. His office always did no matter how large. Names, addresses, relatives, correspondence, conversations overheard, opinions expressed, recorded, cross-referenced and all carefully filed in their allotted place. Always so much. But, then—one could never have enough information.

The Hauptsturmführer sat down at his desk and looked at his watch. Brack's plane would be out over the Channel by now. And von Schreier and his army cronies were safely upstairs drinking themselves into a stupor. The Day was almost over. It had gone well. He opened a drawer and took out the box of cigarettes which his brother, who was with the advancing armies on the Russian Front, had sent to him. Yes—a small reward. A job well done deserved some recognition. A moment of relaxation. The length of one cigarette—no more than that. He struck the match and drew appreciatively on the aromatic Sobranie tobacco.

The generals were drawing up plans for their autumn pheasant shoot when the bomb went off. A muffled roar from somewhere below them: the bookcase tilted and several shelves of leather-bound volumes tumbled onto the floor; the windows shook, and the crystal glasses and decanter trembled on their silver tray. And then there was silence.

As the shouting began, the whistles and the barking dogs, there were hurried footsteps in the corridor outside. The library door opened to reveal the General's secretary.

'Well?'

'An explosion, Herr General.'

'I'm not deaf.' The General got up from his chair. 'Excuse me, gentlemen.'

The dark garden was criss-crossed by beams of light as torches searched this way and that. The tall flames lit up the terrace and the chain of men passing buckets backwards and forwards from the ornamental pond. The group of officers standing at the foot of the steps moved aside as the General approached. Above them, sprawled among the splintered glass and masonry, were two dead soldiers and their dog. A third body, wrapped in blankets, was being carried from the burning room beyond. As it was placed gently on the flagstones two medical orderlies hurried forward and knelt beside it. They spoke quietly to each other and then one of them got up and came down the steps to where the General was waiting.

'The Hauptsturmführer?' said von Schreier.

'SS Hauptsturmführer Honegger is dead, Herr General. And both the guards.'

'Herr General,' called the sergeant, who came running up the path. 'We have found the terrorist.'

They followed him across the lawn to the foot of the boxed hedge. The sergeant rolled the body over with his foot. In the beam of his torch, Ted Naylor's bruised face stared back at them blankly.

'The blast must have caught him as he was moving away, Herr General.'

'An unstable device, Herr General,' observed von Schreier's secretary. 'The work of an amateur.'

'But effective, Werner,' replied the General, 'don't you think?'

'But how did he infiltrate the security cordon?'

The General stooped and pulled open the dead man's jacket. 'So,' he said. 'There is your answer. I suspect this fellow was no stranger to these woods.'

'Herr General?'

'It is a poacher's pocket, Werner.' Von Schreier

indicated the baglike pouch sewn inside the coat. 'I am a landowner—I know such things. What is this?' The General looked up and brushed something from the medalled lapel of his tunic. 'And now more rain?'

Something was certainly falling, drifting slowly down through the darkness. It was everywhere. It was ash: grey, feather-like fragments of burnt paper, charred pieces of filing-card and typewritten pages, floating silently to earth and filling the night air as far as the eye could see.

Frank wasn't sure how long he'd been asleep when the noise woke him. A door slamming? Something like that somewhere outside. He sat up. Rose? It must be Rose coming in late. There'd be ructions in the morning. He settled himself against the pillow. The dream from which he'd been woken was still vivid in his mind:

He was standing by the cottage gate, looking down the lane. And his dad came striding up from the direction of the village. He was wearing his old raincoat, the one that smelt of oil, and over his shoulder was the haversack he always carried his flask and sandwiches in.

'Dad?' he called. 'I've been looking out for you.'

His dad waved. 'Hello, old son!' he replied. 'I hoped you'd be here. Sorry I've been so long. The place is full of Jerries.'

'It doesn't matter.' Frank threw open the gate. 'It doesn't matter a bit.'

And he started running down the lane towards him . . .

Frank frowned. On the ceiling above, the moonlight shining between the curtains had taken on a pinkish glow. It couldn't be morning yet, could it? Dawn already? He slipped out of bed and went to the window. It was there in the sky beyond the village: a dull, rosy light. It looked like the glow from a— It was a fire! And a big one. He could see it above the trees. There was a fire burning in the direction of Shevington Hall. Or could it be? What if? And that sound before, the one

210

that had woken him from his dream? What if that wasn't Rose coming in! He slipped the catch and threw open the window. He could smell it; he could even smell the smoke. It was! It must be the bomb! They'd done it! The bomb had gone off! As he watched he saw lights coming on in other cottages. People were waking up all over the village and hurrying to their windows.

'Frank?' Colin was next to him rubbing his eyes sleepily. 'What is it, Frank?'

'It's all right, Col,' he said. And laughed. 'It's started, that's all. It has! It really has!'

AFTERWARDS

In almost every town and village throughout that part of England which, while the Occupation lasted, was known as the Southern Area Command, you will find memorials to those who died in the struggle against the invader. Men, women, and children of all ages and walks of life who were involved directly in the resistance to the Nazis or who suffered in the reprisals and round-ups consequent upon that resistance.

But among the very first memorials to be erected not long after the Liberation of the area by units of the United States Eighth Army under the command of General 'Ike' Eisenhower in June 1945, was the simple marble plaque set into the flint wall next to the lych-gate of Saints Peter and Paul Church, Middelbury. It reads:

Dedicated to the memory of
The Middelbury Hostages
Murdered by the SS
13 April 1941
Charles Dawson
Matthew Harding
Herbert Jeffreys
Percy Whittaker

and
Edward 'Ted' Naylor
who gave his life for our freedom
22 April 1941
WE WILL NEVER FORGET

It is not unusual, even today, to find fresh flowers have been left beneath it.